THE MAGIC CELLAR
PIGS AND ELVES

Author's Acknowledgments

No child ever had better friends and family than I did. My sincere thanks to all of you for allowing me to tell our story.

To Iva Ellison Case, of Hamburg, Iowa

To Laura Ellison Harmon, of Watson, Missouri (deceased)

To Bill Ellison, of Braddyville, Iowa

To Ernie Ellison, of Watson, Missouri

To Charley Moore, of Watson, Missouri

To Lucille Moore White, of Nebraska City, Nebr. (deceased)

To Irene Moore Dozier, of Oroville, California

And at last, but first in our hearts, a special bouquet to Evelyn Martin Miller, our high school English teacher. Evelyn's command of language and her valued council are like manna to me. With great expectations the final draft of a new book always finds its way to Evelyn's mail box in Ellinwood, Kansas. Will it pass the test? Would "The Magic Cellar" get her approval? After a couple of weeks of hoping, the phone rang. It was Evelyn.

"Colene, I loved it!" she said, and then added, "I am so proud of you." She had given me high marks, thumbs up. We went to press.

So from all of us, to all of you, enjoy!

THE MAGIC CELLAR, PIGS AND ELVES
By
COLENE COPELAND
Illustrations
SHEILA SOMMERVILLE

Manufactured in the U.S.A.
Library of Congress Catalogue
Card number: 95-76659
ISBN: 0-938810-17-4
First Edition

Jordan Valley Heritage House
Publishing Company

THE MAGIC CELLAR,
PIGS AND ELVES
By
Colene Copeland

Chapter 1. The Cellar

The five of us huddled in the darkness, facing the flickering green light, a sort of arch which seemed to outline a door.

Laura heard it first.

"Sh-h-h, everybody. Listen!"

There was a slight rustling, perhaps footsteps. As we watched, too frightened to move or speak, the door slowly opened, ever so quietly.

"Open wide," chirped a tiny little man who stood in the doorway. Was he a man? Perhaps an elf. No, elves are only make believe in books. Aren't they?

"My Queen needs you," he said. "You must come at once."

Surely this adventure was only a dream. Don't all children dream of things as they were, things as they would be, things as they never were and things as they never could be?

It all happened the summer I was ten, the summer I seemed to live two lives, a normal one by day and the other, at night, filled with wonder, worry and excitement.

Of course I was dreaming, I tell myself. Now I am old, but the memories of that special summer are still sharp and fresh in my mind, not at all like normal dreams which become fuzzy and dim and fade away with the dawn.

Perhaps it was magic.

How else can I explain how my playmates and I ventured to an underground city of Great Domes, where a bizarre Queen reigned over her equally strange subjects; a place of little people and Aero Gobbetts, Transit Baskets and Primer Pots, as well as the home of Tackett, our funny little guide.

Suddenly, the dreams, if they were dreams, stopped. Half of my life ceased to exist. I was devastated. Looking back, I can clearly remember the day the adventure ended. It was the same day I declared to whomever would listen, "I am growing up. I am not a child any

more!"

The magic took flight.

Now that I am old, I look back and I question. Was it real? Are magical dreams only for children?

Perhaps if I tell you, you who are still young, you will help me to recognize the truth of it, once and for all.

My story begins either in the potato cellar on our farm in Missouri, or in my dreams when I lived there as a child. When you have heard me out and listened to the entire story, I ask that you determine for yourself which is the truth of it.

Was it dreams? Was it magic? Or was it real?

My friends and I on a summer's day in 1939 ran through my family's kitchen. We slowed down just long enough to pick up a small knife for peeling apples and potatoes. Hearing no objection from my mother, we raced toward the cellar to play.

Noisily, we stomped across the wood floor of the old back porch and down the porch steps. The outside cellar door lay immediately to the right of the steps, handy to my mother's kitchen.

The big wooden door lay almost level to the ground. It took all of us to pull it open. We skipped down a flight of cement steps to an upright door leading into the musty storage room.

The cellar was our favorite place to play. Here, we were in a special little world, known only to us.

But this day promised to be a day like no other child had ever known.

The cellar was completely underground. It was patterned like one of those Quonset huts used during World War II, except the cellar was made of cement. The floor was nearly always damp. The front and back walls were vertical, but the sides and top formed a semi-circle. It was like playing in the top half of a large round tube.

The only light came in through a small ventilation pipe in the ceiling at the rear of the room. The tiny stream of light pointed straight down, leaving the remainder of the room shadowy.

That didn't bother us. We had supplies, plenty of them for any occasion. If we wanted light we could open the door. But we wanted privacy and magic.

Billy struck a match and searched for one of the many candles placed here and there for our use. Soon a tiny light flickered in our little retreat.

Today there were five of us, four of the Ellison kids and me. Iva was nine, Laura eight, Billy was seven and Ernie six years old. Ernie was not the youngest of the Ellison kids.

Beverly was the baby, much too small to tag along. I was the oldest, at age ten. I was Colene Moore then. It was my family's cellar.

"Who is here?" Iva called to the room.

"Who do you think, dummy?" Ernie asked his big sister.

"Don't you feel it? I am not kidding, you guys. I feel like someone is watching us." She glanced around the room.

Perhaps it was because Iva mentioned it. I felt it too. Strange. Except for us, the room was empty.

"Are you girls trying to scare us?" Billy whispered. "If you are you are doing a good job of it. Now, cut it out!"

Though it did not go out, the flame on the little candle flickered. Laura lost no time in lighting a second one.

"What is our problem?" I asked. "We have never, ever been scared down here. Look around guys, it's the same old place. Nothing is different, except us."

Big wooden bins for storing potatoes took up all the space along one side. Sometimes we could smell a rotten tater. Piles of fruits and vegetables were stored in boxes along the opposite wall. Mostly apples. Mama had traded strawberries and tomatoes to some farmer in Hamburg for apples.

Sturdy shelves across the back and part way up one side, by the apple boxes, held the jars of food my mother had preserved from our garden and other food she had traded for. There were hundreds of quart jars of fruit and vegetables as well as several hundred pints of pickles, all kinds.

Mama was always sending me and my sisters to the garden to pick cucumbers for her pickles. She'd say, "Pick me this little basket full of two inch cucumbers for my sweet gherkin recipe." Or, "Pick me a bushel of five inch cucumbers for my dills." Sometimes, she had cucumbers in five gallon crocks out on the screened-in porch where we separated our milk. The cukes were in vinegar and spices. You could smell them half way to Watson.

The half gallon jars contained meat. All kinds. Our family ate well. Mama had been hungry a few times when she was a kid. She swore her children would never know a hungry day. We never did.

"Let's eat something," I suggested, tossing an apple to each of them. "Maybe these apples will 'un-spook' us."

Billy placed some empty fruit boxes in a semi-circle. Four of them, facing the room, backs to the door. I knew what he wanted, because he hadn't provided a seat for me.

"Tell us a story, Colene," Billy urged.

He didn't have to beg. It didn't take much coaxing to get me going. I loved making up stories. I did it all the time. Our little candle lit room was a perfect setting for the wild tales I told.

Now, Ernie began to plead for a story. I was pleased.

I stood in front of them facing the door, trying to look serious. With an uneasy feeling already hanging over us, the stage was set for something sinister. A ghost story perhaps.

I felt a chill, so much so that I rubbed my arms briskly and looked around to see why I felt a slight breeze. Impossible! This was crazy.

Before I could speak something green and brilliant caught my eye. Behind my friends, on the side wall and just to the left of the cellar door, was this odd looking light. What was it? It looked like the frame of a door. I stared at it. My mouth was open but nothing came out.

The Ellison kids turned to see what I was staring at. They, too, saw the strange light. Wooden boxes went flying in every direction. The five of us huddled together in disbelief, too frightened to move.

What did it mean? And who had done this to us?

Chapter 2. Snakes

Some sounds stay with us all our lives. We say, "That is something I will never forget." And we never do.

I will never forget how Ernie reacted. After all, he was the youngest, only six years old. The boy was terrified. His teeth began to chatter, in a loud rhythmic manner. The noise he made with his teeth was the only sound to be heard.

Laura stood frozen next to the cellar door. After a few moments, when she began to think straight, she yanked it open and tore up the steps. The rest of us were right behind her. We pushed, shoved and stepped on each other, like stampeding cows. We **had** to tell our strange experience to someone. **Anyone!** My mother was in the kitchen putting two large loaves of bread dough in the oven of the wood-burning cook stove.

Except for Ernie, we all talked at once. Ernie stared at Mama, his teeth still chattering.

Billy was the loudest. He kept repeating his message, "A door, a door, a strange green door!" Laura's head bobbed up and down agreeing with her brother.

Mama was utterly confused. She had listened to Billy. She got this idea in her head that we had seen a snake in the cellar. My mama was big on killing snakes. She hated them. They slither into the hen house and eat the eggs.

I tried to stop her, but she wouldn't listen. I kept telling her, "We've discovered what looks like a door!"

She dried her hands on her apron, armed herself with her biggest broom and charged out the back door. Pleading in vain, we followed close behind.

Once in the cellar she begin to swing that big broom back and forth like she was dusting the tops of her shoes.

"Where is it, where is the snake?" she asked.

"That's what we've all been trying to tell you, Hattie. There is no snake!" Iva tried again.

"No snake?" Mama asked, looking a little bewildered.

"Mama, nobody mentioned a snake but you. We wanted to tell you about this door." I pointed to what appeared to be a bright green casing around a door.

We kids stood and stared at this strange apparition, feeling calm and somewhat frivolous about it now with Mom there.

Mama would have no part of it. At first we thought she was kidding about not seeing it.

"It's a good joke," she laughed. "You silly kids. Just by standing there staring at the wall you would have me believe that you are looking at a door in the wall. What's next? I've got work to do." She took off up the stairs but turned and gave us one last piece of advice. "Try to stay out of mischief!"

"Do you think she knew about the door already?" Laura asked.

"No, Mama didn't know about it. And she couldn't see it. I could tell," I told them. "I believe this is for our eyes only. Someone or something is doing this."

"It's our magic," Ernie managed to say. "It's just for us kids."

"Surely, Ernie is right, it has to be some kind of magic. What would cause this to happen? Whatever it is, did it suddenly appear by itself?" I asked.

As we stood there in awe of the moment, I was sure I heard footsteps. Iva and I both looked toward the cellar door to see who was coming down the steps. No one was. We looked at each other, both pointing toward the wall.

"It can't be. What would my mother say about this?"

Ernie's poor teeth were taking another beating. It was a very warm day, but Ernie was acting as though he had just come in out of the cold.

"What do you suppose it is?" he managed to say.

"Or who do you suppose it is?" Billy asked.

"Boys, there is nobody behind this wall. It's dirt back there, guys, good old Missouri gumbo." I laughed. "What we heard, or thought we heard was something up on top of the cellar. The dogs and cats are up there all the time."

"Colene, you're trying to make us feel better," Laura said. "But there is something going on behind this door and we all know it."

"And feel it! But you said 'door'. What we have here is a solid cement wall. Sure the light looks like a door frame, but it isn't framing a door." Iva told her sister.

I gathered up the scattered crates and set them upright. Iva opened a quart of Mama's cherry juice. We sat there thinking quietly while each of us took turns drinking from the jar. Nobody took his eyes off those lights for more than a few seconds at a time. Because we were watching, we all witnessed the second manifestation.

Together, we watched. Laura pointed but said nothing. The area outlined by the light began to change color. The total transition took only a few seconds. Before us now was a beautifully carved door minus a door knob. The door was dark in color. In the center was as odd looking crest. Above it, a brass pig. The pig stood upright and wore a crown upon its head.

And now by dear young reader, you must remember something. The year was 1939. There was no television no video games. Today you see things appearing and disappearing all the time. We did not. But because we were together and our friendships were so strong we found the courage we needed.

"Wow! Would you look at that?" Billy stood up and walked toward the door.

"Better watch out, Bill. Hard tellin' what will come through there." Ernie said.

Iva walked around between us and the door. "As soon as we started talking about no door being there, just a light and a cement wall, this happens. We were scared to death of the light. Now we have a door and we aren't so scared."

"I'd say we're pretty brave, wouldn't you?" Billy grinned.

"Well, what do you think we should do?" Laura asked.

"I think we should wait it out. We won't come down here unless we all can come and we'll keep the cellar door part way open just in case we have to run. O.K.?" I suggested.

"I wouldn't come down here by myself, that's for sure," Laura said.

"Let's try something while we're all here together," I said. "Let's turn our backs, close our eyes and count to ten. Maybe all this will disappear and we can forget about it."

"That's silly!" Laura was not in favor.

"Well, I'll try it," Billy told me. "I don't have anything better to do."

When he turned his back to the door, so did we. We counted, one, two, three and then a little faster, four, five, six. We speeded up a little more, seven, eight, nine, ten.

"Open wide," Ernie whispered. Ernie meant for us to open our eyes. But when we turned around we discovered something else was open. **The door.** Seeing the door was one thing, but seeing it open was quite different. Together we stepped near to have a look.

"It's a hallway," I said needlessly, since we all could see for ourselves.

We wondered where it led to, how long it had been there and if we ventured through it, what would become of us?

"Maybe it belongs to the devil," Billy said seriously. He was terrified of preachers and their hellfire and damnation sermons.

"Sorry, I've had enough. I think we need to get out of here." Maybe it was what Billy said, maybe not, but I just wanted to get out of that cellar as fast as I could.

Had we known how badly we were needed beyond that door we would have run down that cobbled stone hallway as fast as we could.

But we didn't know, so we left the cellar. For the next three days we just hung out together. We didn't really say a lot, we just hung out. This time we told no one. It was our secret, and the secret bonded us more closely than ever.

Our families accused us of being up to something. We took long walks out into the fields. Sometimes, we sat in the Mulberry Tree. But always by ourselves. We had to make a decision.

If we chose to go through that door, what would become of us?

Chapter. 3 A Cyclone

In the late afternoon of the third day, dark storm clouds gathered. The wind came up, blowing dust and setting off dirt devils here and there on the ground.

Daddy was discing up an old hay field, so I was stuck with doing the milking. When I was about half finished, my brother Charley, who was twenty-four, arrived in time to give me a hand. "This looks like cyclone weather to me," he said, while we carried the last of the buckets of moo juice to the house.

Mama held the screen door open for us. "I think we are in for a cyclone. The sky gets more yellow all the time." She was shouting above the noise of the storm. "I sure wish your daddy would get to the house." Daddy never came in when it looked like a cyclone was coming until the black clouds began forming a funnel shape. Mama worried about it. Sometimes she'd really scold him for scaring her like that.

"Daddy's coming Mama. Don't worry. He's standing up in front of the tractor seat and bouncing across the dirt clods!" My sister Irene was coming in with a big basket of dry corn cobs for Mama's wood cook stove. As she came in, the screen door blew back and banged against the house.

"Here he comes!" Mama said and would rest easier now that Daddy had come to the house and was all right.

Pointing his finger toward the northwestern sky, Daddy shouted. "Get everybody into the cellar. It's a big twister comin'."

All the chores came to a halt and the Moores headed to the cellar. Daddy and Mama, Charley, my sisters, Lucille who was eighteen and Irene fourteen, me and my dog Nicky, hurried down the steps. Before we got the outside door closed down, our neighbor, Mrs. Frede, her daughter, Barbara and their old bull dog wanted in and so did some fellow from Rock Port who was passing by. My dad knew him.

"Boy, isn't this something, Mr. Moore," he said. "Saw your neighbor running so I stopped to see about her. She told me to get the heck out of that car and head for the cellar, as she was doing. So here we are."

The cellar got pretty crowded with all those grownups and two dogs that didn't like each other.

Right about then I started thinking. All these people would notice our door. Then the whole county would know about it. Too late now! There it was, big as life, and still open!

Mama and Irene lit several candles to prevent us from stepping on each other.

"Mrs. Moore, I've never seen so much food put up in all my life! Did you do all this?" the fellow asked Mama.

"Ain't this something," my dad answered proudly. "Hattie gardens and cans from spring until late fall."

Nobody mentioned the door or the green frame.

Finally, I couldn't stand it any longer. "Do you notice anything different down here?" I asked to anyone listening.

"Like what?" Irene asked.

"You know,--- anything?" I didn't know what else to say.

"You've got to watch out for Colene and the Ellison kids. They get in this cellar and get a little crazy making up stories," Mama laughed. "They got me to run down here the other day to look at a door in the wall. Of course there wasn't any door, just a bunch of silly kids playing tricks."

Everybody laughed thinking we'd played a good joke on Mama. That is, everybody except Daddy. Daddy looked at me in a very strange way.

One thing for sure, we children were right. Nobody could see that door but us. Amazing! Were we special or what? I couldn't stop grinning.

We were used to cyclones and bad wind storms. Nobody was too frightened or said much about the storm, until something large crashed into the outside cellar door.

"Oh my," Mama cried, "It isn't our house, is it?"

Charley looked through a knot hole in the old wooden door.

"No Mom, it isn't the house. It's the privy!" he laughed.

"That's not very funny, Charley!" Lucille said, angrily.

"Are we talking about your outhouse?" Mrs. Frede asked.

"We are," Charley said. "Lucille will have to sleep with a bucket under her bed tonight."

She gave him a dirty look.

After about ten more minutes the storm died down. When we came out of the cellar the first thing we saw was our privy setting upright on the back porch where the wind had put it.

"You ought to take a picture of that and put it in the Atchison County Mail," I told daddy.

"I would be so embarrassed if you did that." Lucille said. "Don't do it, please Daddy." she begged.

"I think we should. Everybody would get a big kick out of it, Lucille. After all, who else do you know that has an outhouse on their back porch?" I teased.

"You guys are sick!" she said, and went stomping into the house.

I knew we'd see a picture of our outhouse in the newspaper. Teasing Lucille is what Charley does best.

The Cyclone

My brother Glenn was two years older than Charley. He married Rebecca Graves, a schoolteacher from Fairfax. They had a farm of their own.

Other than the wind taking our outhouse for a ride, our place suffered very little damage. In the next hour and a half it rained four inches. When the rain stopped it got nice and warm again and brought out the crickets. They made such a racket it was impossible to sleep. By midnight I was so angry I wanted to go out and pull off their legs.

When I finally fell asleep. I dreamed about the place beyond the door.

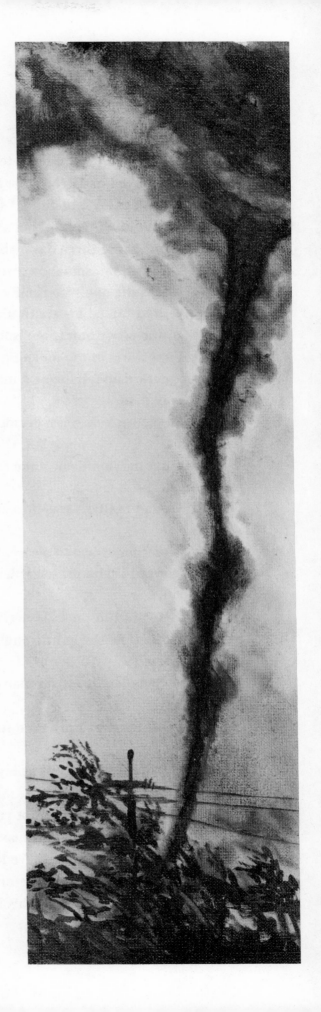

Chapter 4. Tackett

Waiting until morning to tell the Ellison kids about what happened in the cellar was the hardest thing I had ever done in my life. When I finally went to sleep that night, it was so late that I slept in, something I seldom did. But it was too wet for daddy to go to the field to disc, so he did all the milking and let me sleep.

During those three days, since we first saw the door, each of us went through some kind of a transition. Somehow, we all reached the same decision. Even little Ernie.

He was the one who finally said, "I guess we had better check it out."

We had talked at length about what might happen to us if we went through "that door". On the other hand, our spirits soared, wild with curiosity. Anxious and united we agreed. First thing in the morning our plans were to check it out.

A gentle rain fell the next morning. Mama was baking bread. Nobody could bake hot rolls like my mom.

"Mom, we kids have decided to spend the day in the cellar. Can we take food?" I asked.

"What do you mean 'take food'? You kids never get hungry in the cellar, do you?" she grinned.

"No, not really. I was thinking about other kinds of food," I told her, eyeing the hot rolls.

My mother aimed to please. "Well then I guess I'll just have to put some of these rolls in a bag for you. I'd better send plenty. It's hard telling what you'll find down there today," she grinned.

When the Ellison kids arrived, Mama sent Billy to the smokehouse for a bushel basket. By the time she got through filling that basket with food, there was enough for an army regiment.

Billy laughed at my mother because she was having such a good time fixing us that food.

"It will be worth my time just to get you kids out from under my feet today," she teased.

Knowing that we planned to play in the cellar all day, no one would come around looking for us. The day was ours.

Billy pulled the bag of hot rolls out of the basket.

"Don't want 'em to get smashed," he said.

"Sure, Bill," Iva said. "We know why you want to hold the rolls. You'll have your grubby little paws in that bag before we even get down the cellar steps."

Billy smiled and nodded his head in agreement. Billy was a good natured kid and a hard worker for his age. My dad liked Billy as a helper. No job was ever too big for him to tackle.

The basket contained sandwiches of sliced, sugar cured ham, some left over fried chicken, tomatoes, homemade ginger cookies with honey crunch frosting, celery sticks stuffed with peanut butter and a bag of taffy candy left over from my brother Charley's taffy pull party the night before. And of course those hot rolls that Billy was guarding.

There were paper plates in the cellar and plenty of juice to drink.

"Thanks Mom, we won't be home for lunch," I announced, acting silly with my nose in the air. Everybody laughed.

Five brave young souls entered the potato cellar. The candle was not needed. We had left the cellar door partly opened, as planned.

Our secret door was there, but it was closed. So what? We'd wait and see. The green light had grown a little brighter.

The five of us huddled together in the darkness, facing the flickering green light, a sort of arch which seemed to outline a door.

Laura heard it first.

"Sh-h-h, everybody. Listen!"

There was a slight rustling, perhaps footsteps. As we watched, too frightened to move or speak, the door slowly opened, ever so quietly.

"Open wide," chirped a tiny little man who stood in the doorway. Was he a man? Perhaps an elf. No, elves are only make believe in books. Aren't they?

"My Queen needs you," he said. "You must come at once."

He was no taller than the shortest one of us. The pink suit he wore was quite dressy. Small black boots set off his outfit. Perched on his head he wore a tall cone shaped hat, encircled by a narrow brim, that caused him to appear much taller than he really was. And, what looked like a pink cotton ball was stuck to the top of it. Best of all, he wore a broad smile. Nothing was threatening about this friendly fellow. Perhaps that's why we welcomed him so quickly without reservation. I hoped we weren't being foolish children.

"Who are you please?" Laura asked politely.

"I am Tackett, your guide."

The sound of his voice made us laugh. The tiny little man had the voice of a child. Small voice box, I guess.

Years later when I heard a recording made by the Chipmunks, I thought it was Tackett. Alvin's voice reminded me of Tackett's.

But then in 1939, somehow he reminded me of Santa Claus. Perhaps it was because I believed Santa to be some sort of an elf. When I summoned up enough courage I told him

who he reminded me of.

Our little visitor convulsed with laughter. He held his flat little stomach, reared back and laughed loudly. Infecting us all with his glee, we joined in his merriment.

"You are so funny!" I said. "You even laugh like Santa Claus."

"So I remind you of the jolly old elf, huh?" he asked when finally he had regained his composure. "How can that be? Chris is over six feet tall and has a much bigger belly." Again he rubbed his flat little stomach and laughed.

"Oh my, children, here I am laughing and wasting time when I have been sent here on an urgent mission. We can talk on the way. I will answer all the questions I'm sure you want to ask. But we must get started. We are three days late already. I made a promise to Her Highness, I'd bring you quickly."

"Her Highness?" Iva asked. That started it. Questions were fired at the little man so fast, it's a wonder we didn't blow him back down the hallway.

"How did you get so little?" Ernie asked, standing eyeball to eyeball with Tackett. Ernie was six.

"Tell about the lights and the door. How did you do it? You did do it, didn't you," I asked. "What kind of magical powers do you hold? What all can you do?"

"And where do you come from?" Iva asked.

"My new friends, I am a liaison between Her Royal Highness Queen Glory Rose and my people. It is she who sends me to you. It is she who holds the magic. She begs your presence and needs your help. We must go. I hope it is not too late."

Tackett's words surprised us. His Queen needed us. In Missouri when you hear someone needs help, you don't say no.

"We must go now please," he said anxiously. "Her Highness will tell you soon enough why she sent for you." He took a long look around the cellar at the food and at the large basket of victuals sitting there. "Strange indeed that you eat so well without a single Primer Pot." What was a Primer Pot? We had no idea, but we didn't ask. There were more important thoughts in our minds.

I don't know whether it was a child's curiosity or complete trust in a little elf who reminded me of Santa Claus. For whatever reason, he lead the way and we followed him through the door and down the cobbled stone hallway to who knew where.

Chapter 5. Our First Taste of Real Magic

The walls along the hallway were made of dingy grey cement. Many pretty bright lights, shaped like pigs and supported by pink wicker horns of plenty lined the walls.

Laura and Bill carried the basket of food. No reason to leave that behind.

After we had walked the distance of a basketball court the hallway narrowed and turned to the right. Immediately in front of us was a very large glass door. What I saw through that door took my breath away. I had never seen anything so beautiful.

A magnificent coach! Only in picture books had I seen anything like it. But none compared to this. Though there was no light above it, it glowed brilliantly. The coach was built of sturdy looking pink wicker and, ---yes---it was shaped like a pig standing on all four legs. A necklace of fresh pink and white carnations encircled the pig's neck. More flowers formed bracelets around each leg. Fragrance from the flowers filled the air.

Tackett led us through the door and up a couple of steps to the coach. He opened a quaint little pink heart-shaped door and invited us to step inside. I felt like a princess.

Pink, white and lavender pig-shaped jewels lined the walls inside the coach. Soft cushioned seats bid us be seated and be comfortable. A pale pink mist and the sweet smell of the flowers crept around us. We were in awe of it all. Not one of us uttered a word.

Tackett read our faces and smiled at us.

"It is The Queen's magic," he said. Then suddenly he seemed sad. "And just think, soon all this could be gone forever. We must hurry."

Hurry? If he was in a hurry to take us somewhere then why were we sitting there in a pink wicker pig?

Tackett closed the coach door. "Don't be frightened, children," he said, and touched the cotton ball on the tip of his hat. At that moment, things began to happen. Millions of beautifully colored sprinkles of light filled the coach, dancing and twinkling about us. It was pure enchantment!

Was the coach moving? And if so, what made it go? I saw no wheels. I heard no motor. Before I had time to think of other reasons why this pig was incapable of taking us anywhere, I felt a slight jiggle.

The dancing lights slowly waned, but the smell of flowers remained. Was it any wonder? Somehow, we had been transported. We had landed smack dab in the middle of a rose garden.

One by one we stood up and peeked through the cracks between the wicker. Sure enough, we were surrounded by an enchanting rose garden.

The most handsome pig I had ever seen opened the door of the coach and bowed in a charming and most gracious fashion.

"What's this?" Ernie laughed.

Iva poked him pretty hard. "Mind your manners," she warned.

Iva was right. This was a strange place, and **we** were the strangers.

This remarkable pig walked on his hind legs and stood straight up. He was baby blue. I had never seen a baby blue pig. He looked fluorescent, as if there was a light bulb inside of him. He glowed. His hair was soft and thick.

"Welcome," said the pig, in perfect English. "Welcome to the Royal Palace Dome of Her Royal Highness, Queen Glory Rose. My name is Handel and I am very happy to meet you. The Queen is eager to receive you."

Looking at this handsome, baby blue pig was one thing, but hearing him speak, and speak very well, was quite another. We froze in our tracks, as if we were stuck in Missouri gumbo.

"You can talk," Billy's voice squeaked. "I never heard a pig talk."

"These are Royal Pigs, my friend. You'll be amazed at what they can do," Tackett grinned knowingly. He introduced Handel to each of us. Afterward, we were invited to follow this handsome blue pig!

"My orders from The Queen are to bring you directly to her no matter what she is doing," Handel laughed. "And that could be anything. Her Majesty keeps quite busy. No telling where she is. We will beat about for her."

Beat about? I had never heard that expression before.

The garden was alive with pastel colored flowers, mainly pink, dozens of shades of pink, growing on the healthiest green stems and vines I had ever seen. And I had seen lots of flowers in Mama's garden. She even called in to a radio station to get expert advice from The Flower Lady on KMA radio in Shenandoah, Iowa.

Unless I was mistaken, and I **must** have been, these flowers were growing up through purple carpet. Plants can't come up through carpet. Maybe the soil here was purple. Imagine!

Even though we were out of doors in a garden, we were indoors in a giant greenhouse, by the looks of it. Except the roof wasn't glass. It was a rounded Dome, like an upside down bowl. The high ceiling had pictures of flowers of all kinds painted on it.

We passed through a tall vine covered fence by way of a magnificent crystal gate. The crystal was layered and rough with clear objects shaped like circles, squares and triangles caught in between. Wow! Handles on each side of the gate were long thin strips of silver, shaped like pigs standing on their hind legs.

What I assumed was The Queen's palace, came into full view. I expected towers, or at least gables. And moats, drawbridges,---but there were none. This palace did not "show off" or scream out at you. It was nothing like that.

This castle was elegant and majestic, built of white marble. There was a great deal of dazzling gold trim, tastefully used.

And to think, we were honored guests, being escorted in. Iva took Ernie's hand and reminded him to watch his manners.

I wondered if all the plants in the garden were artificial. My daddy always said, 'You gotta have good healthy soil to grow good healthy crops'. I think that includes trees and flowers too.

We followed a carpeted path to the front porch. It was **some** porch, extending the entire front side of the house. Carved columns supported an elaborate roof. Baskets of flowers hung from the ceiling. More huge bouquets adorned the porch floor. Everything was spotlessly clean, freshly painted and properly trimmed. It was lovely.

Just as Handel was about to open the front door to the palace, we heard someone behind us.

Suddenly, from behind a tall camellia bush, stepped a large pink pig, dressed in what looked like Sunday best coveralls. Like Handel, her body, what we could see of it, glowed, as if she, too, had swallowed a light bulb. I believed her to be much older than Handel. Her facial features were not coarse like the hogs on our farm. Like Handel, this pig walked on her hind legs.

When she saw us she smiled and said, "I see you have arrived. Welcome!"

When I turned to the others I saw that Tackett and Handel were bowing to her. Suddenly, we realized that she was The Queen, and that The Queen was really a **pig!** We acted like ill-bred kids and stared.

The Queen removed her hat, exposing a crescent shaped headdress.

We took a stab at bowing. We must have looked foolish.

"Oh children, that is not necessary," she said in the kindest voice. "Show our guests into the main parlor, Handel," she directed.

Laura and Billy still carried the basket of food. The Queen turned her attention to it.

"Why do you carry a basket?" she asked.

"My mother prepared food for us when we told her we wanted to spend the day playing in the cellar." I told her.

Queen Glory Rose smiled a friendly smile. "Then Handel, take them into the royal dining room where they can sit comfortably and partake of a mother's thoughtfulness. I will join you presently."

I never thought I would say it about a hog. But, the old Queen was lovely and graceful. She certainly put the prize hogs at the county fair to shame.

My friends and I were dying to ask questions. So far, we were minding our manners, trying to be good guests without missing anything.

The Queen led the way to the house. As we neared the entrance two young yellow pigs opened the huge double doors and stepped aside. They were dressed in long, black dress coats like Handel's. Real spiffy looking, for pigs. And yes, those yellow pigs glowed too.

Suddenly, I remembered the sugar cured ham sandwiches in our food basket. Did The Queen know? Tackett said it was she who possessed the magic powers. What would she say or do if she knew we ate hogs? Wait a minute! What if these hogs ate humans? I looked around at my friends. Were we being led to slaughter? No, I was being silly. We were invited guests and had been treated with great respect. But we were just kids. Had we been too trusting?

Chapter 6. The Royal Pig Palace

Several medium sized pigs came to The Queens aid. They paid no attention to us. It was obvious they loved The Queen dearly.

"Did you tire yourself, Your Highness?" one asked sweetly.

"Would you like something cold to drink? Perhaps you should consider taking one of us with you to the garden," another suggested.

"Now, now, my dears, don't concern yourself about me. I may be old but I can still help with the work and I do enjoy the garden."

These pigs were gorgeous young females. They too walked upright and wore long dress coats. But theirs were not black. The ones they wore matched their color. One was pink, one pale blue, one pale green, one violet and one yellow. They accompanied The Queen as she ascended the stairs to the second floor.

"When do we eat?" Billy inquired of Tackett.

"The Queen said to take you to her dining room through that big door just ahead. As soon as we get you seated you can eat your food." Tackett obviously knew his way around the palace.

An adult female pig was busy polishing a small area of the floor. She was the first pig I had seen on all fours and I assumed it was because she was working. The floor did not need polishing. It was spotless. Other pigs were here and there cleaning and polishing places that did not need to be cleaned and polished.

The inside walls were also white marble. Magnificent gold and crystal chandeliers hung from the ceiling. Except for the far end, the room was lined with very large, white, cushioned seating. There were several sets of tables with matching chairs.

We were being escorted to the far end, where a long, wide table of dark polished wood awaited us. The chairs had short legs, even too short for us. More pigs came to assist us. We were given pillows for our chairs to raise us up to the table. The pigs were interested in what we were going to eat and where we got it. Other pigs came in to watch us, out of curiosity.

There was no food on the table. However, quite a few large, black, covered pots sat lined up in the center. Whether they had food in them or not remained to be seen.

Placing some of each of the food in front of us, Iva and I emptied the basket.

"I am afraid there isn't enough to go around, but we are willing to share with some of you," I said and felt a little sad about it.

"Oh, we aren't the least bit hungry," a little yellow pig told us. "We just want to see your food."

"You do?" Billy laughed. "It's just food."

The smaller pigs watched and giggled.

"The hot rolls aren't hot anymore, just warm," Billy said.

"Do you want them hot?" Handel asked.

"That **would** be nice," Billy laughed.

Tackett placed his right hand over the rolls and touched the cotton ball on his hat with the other.

"Now try one," he smiled.

Finally, Billy got to bite into one of Mama's rolls. He grinned a silly grin. His face said it all. Tackett had magically heated the rolls.

"How did you do that?" Billy asked. All the pigs watching laughed, as if they were sharing a secret.

Tackett did not answer. But Handal handed Billy a piece of paper and a pointed stick. "Here, write 'hot rolls' on this piece of paper."

Billy was glad the words were small. He knew how to spell both words.

Tackett tossed the piece of paper high into the air. With one hand he touched the cotton ball on his hat and with the other removed the lid from one of the big black pots on the table. The paper floated into the pot and Tackett replaced the lid.

The elf was really enjoying himself. He grinned broadly, rubbing his hands together. He looked at each of us, studying our expressions.

"Remove the lid and all enjoy," he said to all the pigs who were watching the fun.

Each pig took a place at the table. Handel placed an elaborately carved tray by the black pot. One of the girl pigs began to fill the tray from the black pot, with guess what? Hot rolls! They looked just like ours.

We sat there pigging out on our food. Pardon the expression. The others sat with us and enjoyed hot rolls for the first time.

Tackett must be the royal magician to conjure up hot rolls from a cold pot, I decided.

Next, we ate our fried chicken.

"I'll bet you can't get fried chicken from that pot," Ernie told Tackett.

"I wouldn't even try," he said. "We eat no meat."

Handel was listening. "No one in The Domes eats meat. We are happy and healthy diners of fruits, vegetables, grains and nuts."

"In The Domes? What are Domes?" Iva asked.

"You will soon find out," Tackett told us.

"The Queen is coming. The Queen is coming," the younger pigs whispered loudly.

Baskets of flowers were quickly carried in and placed on the long dining table. More were placed about on smaller tables in the room. The fragrance was wonderful.

Her Highness was dressed in a long pink gown. A single strand of large crystal beads hung low around her neck. I thought she looked quite handsome and dignified.

All the pigs stood up and bowed from their middles until she was seated. We tried bowing too, but we weren't very good at it and again felt extremely silly.

With The Queen were those colorful young females who had met her at the door. Now there were a few more of them. They seated themselves near her, across from us.

"Have our guests eaten?" The Queen asked.

"We brought our own lunch," Ernie said, smiling. "But I would like more please."

The Queen smiled back at Ernie. "Then you shall have anything you like. What is your name?"

"I am Ernie Ellison and I'd like a hot fudge sundae. What is your name, ma'am?" he asked.

Iva punched his leg under the table.

"You can't be so informal with The Queen, Ernie. It isn't polite."

"The boy wants to know and it's only fair. I have full reports on each of you. Handel described each of you not by name but by personality, and he imitated each of your voices exactly. If you will each speak your name, I will attach it to your personality, just as I was able to do with Ernie a moment ago."

"I am Colene Moore," I said. The Queen smiled and nodded.

"Yes. You are the motivator. You have a high level of imagination."

As each of the others spoke his or her name, The Queen would smile brightly and comment, "Oh yes, that name fits you precisely."

It was unbelievable. How could Handel have described us so well that The Queen knew us as soon as we spoke?

"Now," said The Queen, "To make things equal, you should know about me, as Ernie indicated."

Can you beat this? Here we were sitting in a palace talking to educated hogs who were wealthier than we were. And now their Queen told us she'd been spying on us, knew all about us! What's next?

Where were we and how did we get there?

I looked toward my friends. I was the oldest and felt I should take responsibility. "I think we had better get going home." But how would we get home?

Chapter 7. The Queen's Problem

Overhearing our talk of going home, Tackett came around to our side of the table looking worried.

"Please, my friends. We have come this far. Her Highness must tell you why she requested your help. I will return you to your cellar in plenty of time. Do not worry."

"We need your help, children," Queen Glory Rose said to us.

"You need **our** help?" I asked. It looked like they were doing mighty fine without us.

"Please let me tell you why," she looked quite desperate.

"Many years ago the wise Elders thought it good to divide up the inhabitants according to their likes and dislikes. The little elves, like Tackett, who live in The Domes are kind, happy and hard working people. But when it comes to governing themselves, they are not very good at it. They are like children. They dislike cleaning and bathing. Left to themselves, they would surely fall into sickness and disease and soon die off.

"We of the royal family are descendants of the Wild Babirusa. Our ancestors were wild hogs. They had tusks that grew so long, they grew back over their heads, resembling horns.

"The wise Elders took pity on the poor beasts. They began to tame the hogs and later, kept them as pets. Eventually, we evolved into tuskless animals and then into teachable animals. At that time the Elders began to educate everyone in our colony.

"Then one day our first Rose Queen mother was born. She was the first with color and with her came the Great Gift. You would call it magic. She was pink, just as I am. She had the first red rose impression on her right hip, just as I have now. She was the first. I am the ninth. Each Rose Queen must give birth, in her late years, to a new heir. I have many children, beautiful children of all colors, but I have failed to give birth to a gifted successor. And I am growing old. "You see children, if I die before giving birth to a new heir, one who holds the magic, the magic will die with me." A lonely tear trailed slowly down her saddened face.

Laura felt compassion toward the aging Queen. "Was the pink basket that brought us here magic?" Laura asked her.

"Yes. That is a Transit Basket. Our Aero Gobbetts, the Primer Pots and much more, all magic," she told us.

"What are goblets?" Billy asked.

"Aero Gobbetts," she corrected. "Tackett will take you on a tour through The Domes in them. First hand, you will witness our problem."

The Queen was desperate! We all felt sorry for her. But as yet I wasn't sure how we could help. Why did she send for us? I asked myself.

"As the builders were tunneling underground they heard your voices in your family's cellar, Colene. A report came back to the palace in regard to the great abundance of food found there and the absence of a Primer Pot. I received that report a long time ago and remembered it. Your food is magically grown. We have never grown food, never had to and we don't know how.

"If our magic dies, my family and the little people will starve to death, **unless**, you children will teach us to **grow** food."

"Oh, we will, we will, won't we guys?" Billy told The Queen. "We all know how. We all help in the garden. We plant seed and pull weeds and everything."

"Sure, we will help you, Your Highness. Your people won't starve to death. Missouri's got no magic and we eat better than anybody," Iva told her. "And we can teach you how to preserve food for the winter, too, like our mothers do."

"My dear, we have no winter. The temperature is always 75 degrees year round, here in The Domes," The Queen told her. Then she turned her head away and signed a mournful sigh. "No, that is not true. The magic will be gone. We shall have winter."

"Don't give up yet," I told her. "There is always hope. That special little pig you are looking for might show up after all. My daddy always says 'The good Lord will provide us with everything we need when he is good and ready'. When I want something real bad and I can't get it for myself I climb way up in our Mulberry Tree. When I reach my favorite branch, I crawl out there and sit and think. I stay there for a long time trying to think of ways I can make the thing I want, happen. That old tree hasn't failed me yet. When we get home I shall sit in my tree and ponder your problem."

The Queen smiled at me, "And I shall be very grateful."

"Everybody in Watson has leftover seed from their gardens," Laura said. "Most of them will just throw it away, unless we go and get it."

"You're right about that!" I agreed, "I know my Mama has seed."

Ernie began to giggle. He was looking at something very small crawling on the table.

"That worm made a face at me," he said, surprised. Soon another worm rolled out from under his plate.

"Dweeds!" Tackett exclaimed. "Pure pests!"

"But funny little pests," The Queen laughed.

"Look!" Ernie shouted. "They have heads!"

The worms, dweeds, were about four inches long and as big around as your finger. Grey and white stripes circled their bodies and their heads were tiny human looking heads. One of the dweeds had short, curly, black hair. The other one was bald.

"That one is called Yul," The Queen pointed to the bald one. "He's a real nuisance.

Please take them outside, Toolee," The Queen requested a young aide.

Toolee was lavender in color and quite attractive. Immediately, she got up to perform the task for her Queen.

Yul jumped on Ernie's shoulder and then dropped down in his shirt pocket. The playful little dweed kept on sticking his head out like he was a jack-in-the-box. Each time his head came up he made a different kind of face.

"Is that all you can do is make faces?" Billy laughed at the silly thing. On the next jump up the dweed spit green stuff on Billy's nose.

"Oh!" Billy shouted, "that's awful!"

Toolee managed to capture Yul. The other one surrendered, quietly.

"I would like to take one of those home for a pet," Ernie grinned.

"Not me!" Billy replied.

With the dweeds gone it was time to get down to business.

"Tackett, it is time now to show our friends through The Domes. Show them what is magic and what is not. Above all else, have them back to their home when they are expected," The Queen instructed.

"Yes, Your Majesty," Tackett responded.

Several members of the royal family escorted us out of the palace and across the garden. They chatted happily and waved goodbye to us as we entered the Transit Basket.

The same familiar fragrant mist filled the air inside. The dramatics began again as the tiny twinkles of light danced about us. Tackett touched his cap and we were on our way and arrived, that quick.

"This is where my people live," Tackett announced happily.

Plainly enough, we had parked in the middle of a narrow little street. Seeing no cars, carriages or horses, I figured we were safe.

One peek through the wicker pig told us it was Tackett's territory. The welcoming committee was out. Dozens of little people held hands, singing and dancing, forming a continuous line around and around the basket.

None of them was bigger than the smallest one of us. They were adorable, especially their children, who looked like dolls.

This was our first taste of celebrity status. Our faces were wreathed in smiles. Tiny, eager hands shoved flowers at us. They touched our arms and our faces in a loving way. The unconditional outpouring of love we felt from these wonderful little folks has never been equaled since, in our lives.

Tackett raised his arms, a signal for them to be quiet for a moment while he

introduced us.

It was obvious to us that our guide was proud of his people. Rightly so.

"These are the children I have delivered to The Queen by her orders," Tackett took pride in his close ranks with The Queen. "Kindly let us pass, please. Our destination, the Gobbetts."

Our arrival was no surprise to the tiny people. However, when Tackett introduced us they said their "oohs and ahs" just like we do when we are delighted about something.

Giving us a path on the straight and narrow street, the elves held on to us and skipped along. A tiny boy held on to Billy's hand, looking up into his face, asking friendly questions.

"Are you a children?" he asked of Billy.

Billy had to laugh. "Yes, I thought I was until I saw you and now I feel pretty big!"

Ernie asked about the road, wanting to know where their cars were. Nobody knew what a car was. Tackett explained that their mode of transportation was the Aero Gobbetts.

It had to be a dream. I pinched myself, hard. Nothing looked familiar to me. Where were we? Was I dreaming?

Chapter 8. The Dome of the Little People

If I was dreaming I could not wake up. If I kept pinching myself my arms might start pinching me back. After all, this was a magic place.

Small colorful, handsomely groomed houses and yards lined the streets. The doors and windows were wide open. Are there no insects to bite the babies or flies to carry in germs, I wondered? I asked the elf nearest to me, a young mother, carrying a baby not more than seven or eight inches long. She had never seen an insect, she told me.

"The only pests we have are dweeds."

A pleasant breeze blew, gentle and warm. Children waved to us from their yards. Were the flowers and shrubs in the yards real or artificial? I supposed they were real. But everything was so---perfect!

The children were very athletic. We watched as they did all sorts of advanced feats of gymnastics. Their body bending, balance and tumbling skills were works of art. Little boys wrestled. Little girls swung on giant swings, just as we do. I wished for a ride, but told myself the swings were made for much smaller children.

Even though we had been told about it, we were amazed to see members of the royal family there doing the cleaning. Two young male pigs worked with the elves replacing a section of the roadway. An older female was painting a trimming of orange vines around a window. We saw several crews cleaning outdoor carpet. The crews contained both pigs and elves, working together.

"I still don't understand why the royal family does all the hard work," I said to Tackett. "It doesn't seem fair to me."

"It would seem fair to you if you understood how much they love doing it. When the deal was made between the first Rose Queen and the Ancient Elders, some haggling took place. The Rose Queens are real smart ladies. I'd say they got what they wanted. The Queens have always loved us and looked out for us. To them, cleaning is a great art, and they then are great artists. Elves don't like cleaning, so the pigs get to do it all, and they love it. That's why we were put together. We need each other."

Laura had a great idea. "Maybe we can get a few of these pigs to go home with us. Billy's room could use some help. Our mother said his room is so full of junk that one day he'll get lost in there and we'll never be able to find him."

Tackett laughed at that. "Billy and my elves have a lot in common!" He grinned at Billy. "I was told to point out to you what is magic and what is not, so you will know what will be taken from us if we should lose the magic. I will be pointing out the difference as we go through The Domes."

Sometimes it was hard to hear each other, because of the elves. Some of them were quiet and listening, but most of them talked and laughed and held on to us.

"So, you want us to teach you how to grow food?" Billy asked.

"After we locate some plots and get the earth turned, we will have to go home for seed," Iva said.

The elves wanted to know what seed was. I tried to explain.

"Seed is like the piece of paper you put in the Primer Pot. But seed is not magic."

My thoughts were interrupted by a grey ball floating from our left to our right, about ten feet above us.

Ernie pointed up, "What is that thing?"

The elves laughed at Ernie's question and obvious surprise.

"You no see Aero Gobbett before?" some fellow asked.

All five of us said it together, "That's an Aero Gobbett?"

Enjoying our ignorance, the elves laughed and jumped up and down.

"Like those up ahead." Tackett pointed out. "Come on. We have to ride in them to locate a garden spot. Each of you choose one."

Up ahead looked like a parking lot for grey balls. So these were the Aero Gobbetts! Each one sat on a tub-like base. Two narrow, glossy metal steps led up to a door.

The little air ships were round, grey, and about three feet in diameter. The front section of the top half was missing. A small door when opened exposed a single seat. There were no controls.

Perhaps it was because we were kids! Perhaps it was because we relished the thrill of riding rides. I'm not sure why we did it, but without hesitation we got on board those peculiar little contraptions, anxious to try one.

"We don't know how to drive these things! We'll fall out and kill ourselves," Billy cried.

A little boy, concerned for Billy's fright, ran up to his Aero Gobbett and said, "Boy, sit down and think thoughts. Cluey tell you right."

"Thanks," Billy said, still concerned.

Tackett called out to us as we were boarding. "What does a garden plot look like?"

"And you are supposed to be our guide," I laughed.

Everybody was too busy having fun to answer his question. For us, it was like a new ride at the carnival.

Up we floated, hovering closely together. Figuring it out was not too difficult. The Aero Gobbetts seemed to read our minds. If we wanted to rise, we rose, if our desire was to go forward, the Aero Gobbett went forward.

Again, Tackett asked, "Please tell me children, what does a garden plot look like?"

"Is somebody going to tell him?" Laura grinned, "Or should we let him guess?"

Tackett loved being teased. The little man felt as though we had accepted him as our friend.

"I'll tell you," Iva replied. "Look for a vacant parcel of land about the size of a large house. Oh, no, that won't work! Your houses are too small! Let's see. How about the size of The Queen's parlor? We can start with one about that size, but you'll need more than one. We can use the first one to teach you how to do it. In Watson, everybody has a garden."

"Everybody?" Tackett looked surprised.

"If you want to eat good food, you plant a garden." Little Ernie said.

"I know a vacant spot, follow me," our little guide announced and led the way across The Dome, through a connecting tunnel and into a second Dome.

How strange! The Aero Gobbetts had no engines or propellers. There was no sound except our laughing and talking as we moved along.

Heavy aromas of cooking filled the air. This Dome was definitely different.

"What is this?" I asked.

"Our Deli-Dome, "Tackett smiled. "You know. Food from the Primer Pots. All kinds. Anything you want."

"Anything I want?" Ernie grinned broadly! He loved to eat!

Laura wasn't too sure about it."Before I eat anything here, I want to check out their pots!" The way she said it made me laugh.

Tackett led the way to a parking lot. It was easy. You got directly over one of those tubs and a vacuum pulled you gently down until you were parked.

Immediately, we were spotted by the elves and became the center of attention. They were curious to see what the food we would order looked like.

The young lady about to take our order became very popular. She was getting to talk to us and by doing so the others held her in high esteem. Seeing that to be so, we tried to be friendly with all the little people. We wanted it known that Missourians are sociable folks.

"We can't order anything. We don't have any money! Do we? Does anybody have any money on them?" I inquired.

"Good," Laura said. "That's a good excuse not to eat this food."

The boys looked at Laura. "Why would anybody want an excuse not to eat?" they were thinking.

Perhaps she was right. There were worms on the table in The Queen's dining room. What would the elves say when they found out we didn't trust their food?

Chapter 9. Carpets and Dweeds

We were in a kind of a predicament! When Tackett noticed we had not yet ordered food, he wanted to know why.

"What if we aren't hungry?" Laura asked.

The little elf laughed. "Not hungry? How can you not be hungry? Just the smell of the food in the Deli-Dome makes me hungry."

"Well, we aren't hungry and anyway we don't have any money," I told him.

"What is money?" he asked.

"I don't know what you call it here, but it is what you use to pay for what you want to buy," I tried to explain.

"Pay? Buy? I don't understand those words and I thought I knew the language just as well as the next elf." He was seriously saddened.

That little fellow, Cluey, the one who told Billy how to handle his Aero Gobbett was there, and began to shake Tackett's shirt sleeve.

"Cluey know. Girl think like trade," he looked at me."You not give to Primer Pot girl anything. Primer Pot girl only give. You eat, smile, not trade."

"I get it, Cluey. The food is free," Ernie understood that. "If this food is free and I can have anything I want, **I am gonna eat**."

The elves looking on applauded Ernie.

Ernie stepped right up to the counter. "I'm sorry, I'm just a kid and I don't know how to spell 'strawberry sundae'. But I would like one, please."

Tackett came to Ernie's aid.

"Do this. Close your eyes, stomp your right foot and give your order."

Ernie tried it. The counter girl reached into the nearest Primer Pot and out come the most delicious looking strawberry sundae we had ever seen.

I was ready to try it. Quickly, I wrote 'hot fudge sundae' on a piece of paper and handed it over. Billy wrote 'root beer float', Iva wrote 'Coke' figuring they wouldn't have it. Laura would not choose. The wait was about ten seconds.

A little white, short legged table was prepared for us. The elves pulled out our chairs for us and stayed around to watch. Tackett's food was familiar to them but not to us. It was composed of a lot of great looking fruit piled inside of a larger fruit resembling a scooped out pineapple.

Billy told us to look up. I thought there was an Aero Gobbett going over.

"At what?" Ernie asked, seeing no Aero Gobbett.

"Just look, guys."

We looked. Billy had spotted advertisements pasted on the ceiling of The Dome. I guess they were advertisements. But why would anybody advertise when everything is free? There were very few bare spots. Pictures of fruits, vegetables and tempting looking dishes. The soft drink signs were the most colorful. The pictures of candy looked like real candy.

In Missouri there were billboards advertising cigarettes and beer. I didn't see any here. In fact I hadn't seen anyone smoking or drinking beer. Those little people and even the pigs were smarter than a lot of Missourians.

Musicians were about to liven up the area. Coming toward us, up the narrow street, was what looked like a mustard colored gypsy wagon, decorated with flowers and lanterns. But it wasn't. It was a traveling stage. Everything attached to it either banged, or clanked, bonged or tinkled.

A couple of dozen elves pushed and pulled on it. By the looks on their faces, they were enjoying the job.

Only one side of the wagon was open to expose a perfect stage for small entertainers. Tiny lights were embedded in vines and yellow rose buds framing the stage. Lots of long icicle shaped crystals hung from the ceiling chiming like tiny bells.

By this time it should have been an impossibility to surprise us. However, when we took a look at the entertainers we were surprised!

"Are they leprechauns?" Iva asked.

Now it was Tackett who looked surprised. "You know about leprechauns?"

"Sure, we can read you know," Iva told him. "But these little fellows are elves, pretending to be leprechauns. Right?"

"No. They visit us every now and then from the Emerald Isle," our guide informed us. "We love their music and songs."

There were six little men, no taller than the full grown elves here in The Domes. But the leprechauns were skinny and had wrinkled faces like they had stayed out in the sun too long. Their suits were green satin and very impressive. Their shoes were the customary green satin with turned up toes. Each shoe had a darker green shamrock for a buckle.

"How did **they** get here?" Billy asked the question on all our minds. "Did they just dig a hole and drop in?"

"We found them, the same way we found you. What a treat it was to find folks our size who entertained and were willing to travel. They come often."

When they began singing we almost died laughing. Irish songs here in The Domes? Who would believe it? First it was "My Wild Irish Rose." I wondered how The Queen felt about that one. Then it was a funny little song sung in Ireland in pubs. They were very good.

The elves looked to see if we were enjoying the music. We were. In fact Billy got up and danced an Irish jig right there by the table. The leprechauns loved it. A couple of them jumped off the stage and danced with him, for all to see and enjoy.

"Where did ye learn ta jig, laddie?" one of them asked of Billy.

"My teacher, at school, she taught us," Billy smiled broadly. He was loving the attention.

"Was her hair as red as flame?" the little man asked Billy, in a wonderful Irish brogue.

"Yes sir! Red as flame!" Billy answered.

"She be one of ours then," he said happily. He then hopped back up on the stage. He pointed a bony finger at Billy, "For you," he said, grinning. All but one of them joined him in a lively, high stepping jig. The one remaining accompanied them on the flute.

We finished our delicious treats. Hard to believe they were as good as the ones we bought from I.B.Gaines's drug store in Watson.

A young girl, an elf, washed the dishes, but the cleaning of the table, even the chairs, were eloquently and artistically wiped clean by pigs.

We said goodbye to everyone and thanked them. Then it was back to business and up in the Aero Gobbetts searching for a place to plant the first garden.

More acquainted now with our surroundings, we relaxed and enjoyed the funny little advertisements on the ceiling and the cute dwellings below us.

Another Aero Gobbett floated along beside us, the funniest thing we ever saw. It was covered with dweeds. Dweeds were hanging on around the outside and all over the top. For several minutes they moved along with us and entertained us in a way we had never been entertained before, or since.

They made ugly faces at us, ridiculous faces. They laughed and made purring sounds and cat calls. Oddly enough, some of them had painted their faces like clowns. One blew up a balloon with words written on it. It read, "I am Cloclo the clown-o, if you don't like my face you can kiss my tallywago!"

"What's a tallywago?" Billy asked.

Tackett blushed. "Don't ask. The dweeds are naughty!"

"How can a worm blow up a great big balloon like that one?" I asked.

"Dweeds can do anything they want to. The blasted things are smart!" Tackett told us.

The worms stood on each other's heads. They shook their hiney's, or at least what looked like hineys, at us, while purring out silly little tunes, savoring every minute of it. They sang this song.

Come a little closer, take a better look,

We'll poke out your eyes and grab you with a hook.

Carpets and Dweeds

We'll bite your funny butts and
spit on you with dye,
When you think we're finished,
we'll blow you from the sky!
Hee, hee, hee!

Twice they sang their song before dropping quickly out of sight.

"I haven't decided if I like those worms or not," Laura frowned. "I have an idea they could cause us real trouble if they wanted to."

Perhaps she was right. Had we, or had we not seen the last of them?

Chapter 10. Strange Vets and Dirt

Tackett pointed below and to our left. "There's the spot I'm looking for!" Immediately, our Aero Gobbetts circled and headed in that direction. Incredible!

Below us lay a large vacant lot, covered with lush green grass, the first grass we had seen. Plowed under, the grass would provide fertilizer for the new seed.

We made use of a parking lot near the grass.

Iva was the first to reach the vacant lot. "What is this?" she exclaimed. "This isn't grass, it's carpeting!"

"Carpeting?" I asked. "Why on earth would anybody carpet a vacant lot?"

"At least, I think it's carpeting! But it looks exactly like grass!" Iva responded.

"Maybe on earth, nobody would carpet a vacant lot! But here in The Domes, The Queen will have no dirt exposed. She orders everything carpeted." Tackett explained.

"But dirt is dirt and soil is different," I told him. "Our great ol' Missouri soil is what feeds us."

"This carpet will have to come up," Iva told Tackett.

"The Queen won't like it!" he said nervously.

"Then your Queen is going to get mighty hungry," Billy said. "No soil, no garden. You can't have one without the other."

We felt a little sorry for Tackett as he stood there looking quite helpless.

"Then we had better go right away and tell The Queen," he said sadly.

Silently, we took the Aero Gobbetts back to the Transit Basket and the Transit Basket back to the royal gardens.

The garden was busy with activity. An immaculate white bench was setting still for another unneeded coat of paint. An older female hog picked dead leaves from a plant and placed them in a purple basket. Another cleaned an area of artificial turf. A white, adult male hurried around from worker to worker, smiling, as if he was telling good news.

Again, Handel met us. He was wearing the same black coat and a big smile.

"There will be celebrating tonight," he said. "And lots of singing and dancing."

"What is the occasion?" we asked.

"Anna Anessa has given birth to a veterinarian!" he announced proudly.

We all laughed thinking it was a joke. But by the look on Handel's face, it was no joke. I think we hurt his feelings.

"I'm sorry, Handel, we don't understand. In Missouri a person is not born a veterinarian. First he grows up. If he wants to be a veterinarian he goes to college to learn veterinary medicine," I told him.

"How odd," Handel replied as he led the way into the palace.

As soon as the Rose Queen learned of our return she came downstairs to greet us.

"Have you heard the good news?" she asked.

"Yes, but somebody better explain it to us. How is it possible for a pig to be a vet the moment it's born?" Laura asked, in disbelief.

"Did you get to see our Fitness Dome today?" she asked.

"No, we did not!" Laura answered, waiting for an answer to **her** question.

"My dear young friends, we who live in The Domes take great pride in our good health. We eat good food, keep everything clean and get lots of exercise.

"Our veterinarians are from our royal family. Our medical doctors who care for the elves are also from the royal family. When a new white pig is born, such as the one today, its destiny has already been foreordained by the Ancient Elders. The whites are loving and caring and extremely brilliant. In less than a year this newborn pig will be a doctor of veterinary medicine. The pig's training began before it was born."

"That little girl pig is going to be a vet?" Ernie laughed.

"Yes she is. Isn't it wonderful!" The Queen smiled at Ernie.

"I've never heard of a girl vet before. Course I never heard of a pig Queen either!" Ernie joked.

Remember it was 1939, a time when there were very few lady vets.

The Queen laughed out loud, knowing full well it was not a dignified thing to do. But she liked Ernie and his honesty.

Queen Glory Rose told us we were the only humans she had ever seen, although her mother had seen one long ago. She admitted to being worried before we arrived.

I don't know how they did it but the tunnel builders who discovered us learned a great deal of factual information and inside dope about us and how we lived. The Queen told us so, including the fact that we not only ate pork, we enjoyed it! No wonder The Queen had her doubts about us. I vowed I would never again eat pork. And I never did.

"Your Majesty," Billy tugged at The Queen's clothing. She **was** tall and he felt awkward trying to talk to her. We all did.

As if she understood his discomfort, ever so gracefully the Rose Queen dropped down on all fours and smiled at Billy.

Suddenly, Billy broke the news to her.

"If you want to grow food, you've got to uncover some dirt!"

The word "dirt" slapped The Queen's ears with a sharp blow.

"What?" she exclaimed loudly. "Uncover dirt? Never! Impossible! Dirt is for the dirty and sick." She stood up tall and proud and held her ground, so to speak! "Our homes are

impeccably clean. We are born into cleanliness. Dirt is an enemy and we are victorious over it. Any dirt, dust, garden trash and garbage is hauled outside The Domes to the cavities in the ground. The hauling wagons and their drivers are sanitized before being allowed back inside."

"But Your Majesty!" Iva pleaded, "look at us, we aren't dirty! Our soil isn't covered up with carpets!"

"And we are healthy," I added. "Everything we eat comes from our soil. I've never heard anybody complain about it being dirty. My dad says our soil is rich and healthy and will grow anything and he is a very smart man."

The Queen was astonished. "How can that be?"

"If you will notice, we call the ground for growing, 'soil'. Dirt is definitely different," Laura tried to explain.

"Well, sometimes I fall down and get dirty, but it doesn't matter. My mother makes me take a bath every night," Ernie laughed.

"Who cleans all that carpet?" I asked, thinking it was such a waste of time.

"We do!" The Queen answered.

"Well, Your Majesty," I told her, "If you won't uncover the soil, then we can't give you a garden. It's as simple as that! We are fresh out of magic tricks. Where we come from, you either grow food, or go hungry!" I turned to Tackett who was standing, listening. "You might as well take us home. Our families will be expecting us to come out of the cellar to do our chores."

The Queen motioned for him to do as I asked. We waved a weary goodbye and left her presence.

Our journey back was swift. Why would such a wise Queen ask for our help only to deny it?

"You have presented my Queen with strange new ideas." Tackett told us. "She must ponder what you have said. No doubt you will see me again," he said, as we parted at our secret door in the cellar.   He was gone. Would we ever see him again?

Chapter 11. Waiting

The little alarm clock on the cellar shelf alerted us that our return home was none too soon. The Ellison kids hurried home and I headed to the barn to help Daddy with the milking. After that, I pumped a couple of buckets of water from our old well to fill the reservoir in Mama's woodburning cook stove. The stove warmed the water, enough for us to use to wash our faces and hands, and we used some of it to wash the dishes. For scalding the dishes, we used boiling water from the big teakettle on the stove. Irene wasn't there to do her chores, so I got stuck with those, which were to carry in two bushels of dry corn cobs and several armloads of small kindling for Mama's cookstove. If we wanted to eat, we had to take good care of Mama's fuel supply.

By the time I finished, supper was on the table. Mama was a good cook. For supper we had pork cutlets. I had to pass them by. But I had mashed potatoes and gravy, sliced tomatoes, fresh from the garden, fresh mustard greens, also from the garden, deviled eggs, fresh from our henhouse. Last but not least there were hot rolls and country butter. A pitcher of milk and one of lemonade sat on the sideboard. I hated milk.

My sisters, Irene and Lucille, did the supper dishes.

Mama had gone to the henhouse to gather the eggs from the nests.

I followed my dad into the living room. It was Saturday night. He had already been to town and bought the Sunday St.Joseph News-Press and Gazette newspaper and the usual big bag of candied orange slices. My plan was to get to Daddy before he got into his paper. I needed time for all the questions I planned to ask. So I tried my hand at being tactful, something new for me.

"This old farm sure feeds us good. Don't you think so, Daddy?" I asked.

He smiled at me and answered,"Uh, huh."

I kept on, "I guess we have to thank our good old Missouri soil? Right, daddy?"

Daddy sat down in his favorite chair in front of the radio. He put his glasses on. But before he could turn the radio on or reach for his newspaper, I got down on my knees by his chair and took hold of his hands.

"Yes, we do eat good. Hard work and good soil, that's about all it takes," he said.

Good for me, he mentioned soil. Now for the big one. "Daddy, is there any way a person can grow food without soil?" I asked.

"Why?" he laughed. "Do you think we are gonna run out of soil?"

"But what if you wanted to grow something without soil?" I asked.

"Little girl, you are asking some mighty foolish questions! Go play, and let me read my paper," he begged.

I still had not let go of his hands. "But Daddy, I want to know!" I pleaded, not wanting to leave him until I had gotten satisfaction.

He must have sensed that. I knew he wanted to get rid of me so he could rest.

He got up and led me to the big mahogany bookcase that divided our dining room and living room. Quickly locating a large, green, well worn book, he handed it to me.

"Here, look in the index for what you want to know. This book can tell you everything you need to know about growing food." He turned to head back to his chair, but stopped, like a magical switch jogged his brain. Returning to the bookcase, he came up with a small pamphlet the size of a comic book.

"You might read this," he said, with a kind of mischief in his eyes. The little book was entitled 'The Wonder of Worm Castings'.

"What's this?" I asked.

"You'll see. Read it and see if you can come up with your own ideas about making good growing soil." With that bit of advice he finally sat down and turned on the radio, to the news.

Although Daddy's help didn't take much effort it was doubtful I had been given anything helpful to The Queen's problem.

By folding back a section of the lace table cloth on the dining room table, I had a place to study. I'd begin with the small book about worms.

Reading was one of my favorite pastimes, so I read pretty fast. When I began I was sure both of the books would be boring. Was I wrong! In less than an hour I had totally devoured Daddy's worm book. From now on I would have more respect for worms.

Earthworms look the same on both ends. They are headless, eyeless and toothless. They don't even have antennae or feelers, but they must have mouths. Somehow they eat the soil and everything in it. The soil is digested and conditioned as it passes on through their bodies. It is then referred to as "castings". These castings are far richer in minerals than the soil the worms eat. Their digestive system is equipped with a gizzard-like organ. I thought chickens were the only creature with gizzards.

Researcher Charles Darwin found that the amount of soil these creatures pass through their bodies each year can be as much as fifteen tons of dry earth an acre. The digestive juices of the earthworm make the soil's organic matter and mineral content more valuable to plants. Their castings make excellent fertilizer.

Earthworms are very useful and highly rated for their work in aerating, mixing, and draining the soil.

Daddy always said, "Where you find earthworms present, you find good soil". And my daddy always knew what he was talking about. Here is another thing he taught us about worms that works every time. If you need a can of worms quickly for fishing, go pick up an old board or a bucket that has been setting in one spot for a while. You will find plenty of fat ones for Missouri River catfish fishin'.

All of this information about worms caused me to wonder. What about the dweeds? I thought they were worms. In fact, I knew they were worms! How come they had heads? I sure wished I could ask Daddy about dweeds. I wondered what he'd say.

Mama stopped by the table to see what I was reading. She stood behind me and rested her hands on my shoulders.

"Worms? Soil? When did you become interested in soil?" Mama asked.

"You know how it is when you get interested in something and can't wait to learn more about it?" I said and hoped it was convincing.

Mama didn't answer. She cranked her head around in front of me and gave me a funny look.

"Listen to me, Mama. Is there a way to grow food without soil? Would we starve?" Even if we never saw the Rose Queen again, her problem was the only thing on my mind.

"Ask your sister," Mama said.

I didn't understand. "What do you mean?"

"Ask Lucille about it. Her ag class visited the experimental farms in Iowa last fall. She saw tomatoes being grown in water."

I rushed to find my sister. Mama was still talking to me, but I was finished listening before she was through talking!

Did she have the answer to our question? My sister? There really was a method of growing food without soil or "dirt", a word that sickened The Queen.

Lucille was getting all gussied up to go out with one of her boy friends. She smelled great. The white summer dress she and Mom had made looked nice on her. She wore red shoes and beads and was deciding on earrings.

"How do you like these?" she asked, turning an ear in my direction.

"Perfect!" I told her casually, wanting to get on with it. A corn cob hanging on a wire would have gotten a "perfect" from me!

"Mom said you learned how to grow food without soil when you went to Iowa last fall. How do they do that?" I asked.

She ignored my question completely. "How do you like my dress? I hope Carl likes it."

"Your dress is great! Come on 'Ceel answer my question." I pleaded.

Glancing at her backside in the full length mirror on the back of our bedroom door, she adjusted her belt.

"Why are you interested in hydroponics? Daddy would never let you mess around with it. It's too expensive!" she snipped, knowing I was always fooling around, trying new ideas.

"Tell me about it anyway," I begged. "About the hydro whatever."

"When I get back tonight, if you are still up, I'll let you look at the brochure they gave me at the college," she replied, still primping.

I wondered if Carl was worth all the bother.

I pressed my hands together prayerfully and looked into her eyes. "Where is it?" I begged.

Was I really this close to finding help for The Queen? Or was it possible her own stubbornness would cause her kingdom to self-destruct?

Chapter 12. Talking it Over

"Where is what?" my sister asked, dreamily.

"The brochure, the one on, ---you know,"

"O.K.! If it can't wait!" she laughed. After taking down a large shoe box from the top shelf in our clothes closet and thumbing through a pile of papers, she handed me a white, folded brochure with a big red tomato on the front.

"Here, you can borrow it Sis, but please return it to this box. O.K.?"

I agreed. I felt like giving her a hug. So I did! After which, she checked herself to see if I had messed her up any. How rude! Not nice!

I couldn't believe it. Was it possible that this information was the magic we needed to save Queen Glory Rose and all the Dome dwellers from starvation? I wanted to tell my friends! The big striking clock on the wall in the dining room made it past 8:30, too late to go to Ellisons. I ran to the front window to see if there was a light in Iva's and Laura's bedroom. There was. But just as I crossed our front porch, the light went out. They had gone to bed. Elsie believed in putting her kids down early, so she could get some rest.

I felt disloyal to my friends, as I read the brochure alone.

Three times I read the information on hydroponics. The more times I read it the more disappointed I became. Lucille was right. It was too expensive. And, if it was too expensive for farmers, it certainly would be too expensive for five kids.

Seeds and plants are set into sand or gravel, or most anything that will support the plants. Slanted growing trays allow a constant flow of water and nutrients to pass through the plants and seed. Nutrients are liquid fertilizer. Liquid fertilizer is so expensive my dad wouldn't even buy it, so, how could five kids with no money afford it?

I glanced through the big green book Daddy had given me. "What's the use?" I said to myself. If The Queen won't let us uncover her soil then she's out of luck. My guess is, we will never know, since I was sure we had seen the last of her. I felt like crying.

I put the books away and straightened the table cloth. By then, Carl had come and gone with Lucille. Mama didn't like Carl very much. Daddy and Mama said a Baptist would be a better choice. Irene was washing her hair. Daddy was listening to the Grand Old Opry and a lot of static on the radio. That same old guy was singing "The Great Speckled Bird" again. Mama was looking through her pattern box. I went to bed.

The next day, playing in the cellar was definitely out of the question. It was Sunday. Children in our community attended Sunday School and preaching services. The rest of the day we were expected to visit with our family and relatives. Mama was big on family get-togethers on that day. On Sunday, the only work we were allowed to do was to feed the livestock and milk the cows.

Monday morning took a long time getting there. At ten, not a moment later, we were back in the cellar.

After we talked for a while, Ernie began to cry.

"We'll never see that old Glory Rose pig again," he blubbered.

Laura didn't help matters any when she said, "I don't want to go back there if we have to watch them all starve to death!"

Ernie cried even louder.

"Please don't cry, Ernie," I told him.

Billy put his arm around his little brother trying to console him. "That old Queen, even if she is a hog, is pretty smart. She really does care about the little people and her family. Things will work out all right. She will figure something out. Why that little Tackett will show up here any time now and let us plant those gardens. You'll see."

Laura was full of gloom and doom. "But what if she won't let us take up that carpeting, and what if she doesn't give birth to a magical baby? Then what?"

"What if, what if, we don't know anything for sure!" Iva was irritated with her sister.

"Right," I agreed. "Billy, why don't you take your brother out and climb the Mulberry Tree. Forget about The Domes for a while."

"Good idea," Laura grinned, "I think I'll go with them."

With the three of them out of our hair, Iva and I had a chance to talk at length about the most unusual problem ever faced by five kids. I told her what I had learned from Daddy's books and my discovery of hydroponics. We agreed as great as it sounds, hydroponics was not the answer.

Iva had spent her evening scouting for garden seed. Everybody in Watson grew vegetables.

"I just asked if they had any leftover seed to donate to some families who need help this year," she laughed. "I had to be careful though. Everybody wanted to know if they could help with anything else and who it was. I told them it was a family my mother knew and she didn't want me to give out their name. I sure hope they don't ask my mother."

"Iva, where do you think we were? Where did the Transit Basket take us?" I asked.

"I don't know, Colene, but wasn't it wonderful? Everything happened so fast. We spent most of the time with our mouths open, just gawking," Iva laughed. "No one would ever believe us. Floating along in the Aero Gobbetts, little space ships that were operated by our thoughts and wishes. I can hardly believe it! And I was there!"

"Have you thought about the builders locating this potato cellar? That tells me they aren't too far away." I said.

"On the other hand, they could have come some great distance to get here," Iva answered, while juggling three large russet potatoes in the air. "I don't think they tell time and distance the same way we do."

We talked and giggled and giggled and talked some more about our experiences with the elves and the royal family. So much difference between these hogs and our farm hogs. Imagine, the smell of roses instead of the smell of pig pens. Our farm hogs acted like hogs. They ate field corn and pasture, walked on all fours, definitely did not talk to us, wear clothes, nor show any concern at all when their bodies were muddy. How enchantingly different the royal pigs were. They were beautiful and intelligent. To think, we talked *with* them not *to* them.

Iva and I enjoyed our chance to talk alone. Actually, this had been our first opportunity.

We talked about another peculiarity we had noticed but not discussed, and that was the physical features and clothing of the elves.

The little men wore pink. Pink britches and vests, pink Robin Hood type hats, and shiny black shoes with brass buckles. We laughed about the men wearing pink. Here in Missouri it was considered sissified for a man to wear pink. He would be laughed at.

Another thing I must tell you, though I hesitate for fear of sounding uncomplimentary. The little men were very homely. Had an unsightly plague been visited upon them? To be quite blunt, as Billy put it, "They look like they've been hit with an Ugly Stick!".

Most of the men were quite tubby, with round ruddy faces that clashed with the color of their clothing.

But here was the most amazing thing, the little females were gorgeous. Most of them were quite slender and had faces like dolls.

Flowers, lace and lots of ribbon adorned very stylish green dresses and bonnets. They wore only green, but many, many shades of green. I couldn't remember what kind of shoes they wore, probably because I was too busy looking at their faces. I'll bet we stared.

How strange and unfair it was! The girls got all the looks. Maybe nobody ever told them the men were homely. They were a happy people who laughed and played. And to think, they might cease to exist! The thought was painful indeed.

Chapter 13. Wind and Waiting

My mother called to us from outside the cellar. "How many for lunch today? I'm making potato soup and ham salad sandwiches."

"Are you sure you want to feed all of us?" Iva asked.

"Sure," Mama answered. "I'll phone your mother. She'll be glad to be rid of you a little longer," she laughed. She heard the other kids up in the Mulberry Tree. The tree was huge, full of lush leaves and fruit. Their talking gave them away.

"Shake down some Mulberries for the hens, kids," Mama called.

"Them old hens will be laying blue eggs, Hattie," Billy hollered back.

"They'll still fry, won't they, Billy?" she laughed. "Maybe we ought to put some of their eggs under an old hen to see if she will hatch out blue chicks. Wouldn't that be something?"

"That would really be something," he giggled and began shaking the branches. A shower of berries fell from the heavily ladened branches, scaring the chickens. When some of them got bopped on the head, they ran for cover. But when the shower stopped they sauntered back to eat, with one eye focused on the kids.

Tuesday and Wednesday were normal days. Occasionally one or two of us ran to the cellar and stayed for a minute or two to check for a sign of a door, or Tackett. Neither materialized. Thursday came and went, and so did the next week, and the week after. As the days passed without word, our fears mounted.

I did as I had promised The Queen, which was to sit in my Mulberry Tree and ponder her problem. Was I wasting my time? Probably.

The greater part of the time found the five of us together, talking or deep in thought. We shared our secret with no one. Our families guessed something was wrong, but we denied it.

But something happened we had not planned on. Ernie became ill. George and Elsie heard him crying out in his sleep, "Glory Rose, Glory Rose, please don't die!". Even during the daytime he would go off in a corner alone, sobbing pitifully.

"Ernie is having nightmares," Elsie told my mom. "He is dreaming about some girl named Glory Rose. I don't know anybody by that name, do you, Hattie?" Mama shook her head, no.

"I've asked the kids," Elsie continued. "They say, 'don't worry about him, Mom, he's having a bad dream'. But I do worry about him. He's got us puzzled. Doc Gray said there is nothing physically wrong with him. He asked if Ernie had been through some kind of a traumatic experience. Can you believe that? If he has, what was it?"

Iva and I were on the back porch listening to every word and feeling guilty for getting

Ernie involved in our strange adventure. If we had tried to get Ernie to stay behind, that kid would have pitched a fit. We knew exactly what was wrong with Ernie, but trying to explain it to our parents was out of the question. Ernie was grieving over Glory Rose. He was thinking she was dead already and that was why we hadn't been sent for. We tried everything, but nothing we said or did, helped. We had heard of people grieving themselves to death. We prayed to God it would not happen to Ernie!

My mother had her own idea. "All I know is, something is going on. The kids are so secretive. They stick together like glued flies. When I walk within earshot of them, they stop talking. Let me work on Colene. I've never known her to keep secrets from us."

That night we had another Missouri wind and rain storm. In the late afternoon the dark clouds turned out en masse. Lightning split the sky and thunder rolled and growled. Possibly, a cyclone. As dusk fell the sky was as black as midnight and it stayed that way.

Mama lit the kerosene lamps in the house, so we could see. I was eleven before we got electricity. But as fast as Mama lit the lamps, Daddy blew them out.

"We're going to the cellar," he shouted. "Come on everybody, be quick about it."

As we reached the cellar door, the wind blew Daddy's straw hat off and lifted in up over the fence and into the chicken yard. I hoped it would land on a chicken's head, but the chickens had already run into the chicken house for safety. I didn't think chickens had that much sense.

The cellar was the safest place to be when high winds and cyclones came through, sometimes blowing off roofs and flattening buildings.

The wind always picked on our outhouse. I told you about the time the wind blew it across our cellar door and left it resting upright on our back porch. Lucille sure was angry when she saw a picture of it in the newspaper. Her friends teased her, just like my brother Charley knew they would when he had it put in there.

The year before, the wind took our outhouse off in another direction. Daddy found it a few days later out by the railroad tracks that go through our farm. Flave Gaines, one of our friends who worked on the railroad, asked my dad if he was missing an outhouse. Daddy told him we were. Mr. Gaines told him where it was.

We already had a new one built and in use before we found out what happened to the old one. An outhouse was something a person could not do without.

While we waited out the storms, the minutes always seemed like hours. Half the town of Watson had cellars and were in them. The other half was wishing they had a cellar to get into.

Our house was the first house outside the city limits, yet we were only three blocks from Main Street. Watson's population was about 400.

My Dad and Mom, Irene, Uncle Arley who was Mom's brother, my dog Nicky and I were in the cellar. We sat around and waited and listened to the storm. Mama was scared of this one.

I was the one who lit the kerosene lantern and I was the one who arranged boxes to sit on. I claimed the cellar. These were my guests. "Wouldn't it be wonderful if, right now, Tackett would show up?" I thought. But he didn't.

When the wind quieted down, everyone filed up the steps. I brought up the rear. As I was about to step through the upright door I glanced at the wall where the door had come and gone. The faint outline of the green frame blinked at me---a signal.

I was so happy, I cried! That meant they were still alive. All was not lost. First thing tomorrow we would check it out.

Daddy said going to Ellison's was out of the question. The rain was coming down in sheets. He said too, I'd get blown away. I wasn't a child who disobeyed my father. I had too much respect for his judgment. I could always telephone. So, when no one was listening, I went to the phone on the dining room wall. I asked Mrs. Bowers, the switchboard operator to ring George Ellisons for me. She did.

Laura answered. "Did you guys go to the cellar?" she asked.

"Yes, and it's green arches," I told her. I had to be careful, switchboard might be listening.

"Really?" She was as excited as I was and couldn't wait to tell Iva and the boys, especially Ernie.

"First thing in the morning?" I asked.

"We'll be there," she said, and hurried to tell the news.

Later that evening I was trying to act normal by cutting out paper dolls from a Shirley Temple cutout book. Mom must have read my mind. She made a great suggestion.

"I'll pack a nice lunch for you kids tomorrow if you will spend the day with Ernie. Try to cheer him up, poor little fellow. He looks so unhappy. How about it?"

"Sure Mom. I feel sorry for him too. We'll see if he will play in the cellar and tell stories and stuff. He likes that," I told her.

"Thanks honey," she said, as if I were doing her a favor.

When morning came things looked bleak. Ernie was not allowed to come out to play. He was too sick. Dr. Gray had told George and Elsie to take Ernie to Kansas City to a specialist. Day after tomorrow, they'd go by train.

Ernie's brother and sisters had done a lot of talking to him. They tried telling him we may have imagined Glory Rose. But Ernie wasn't buying it.

Ernie was keeping our secret, except when he talked in his sleep. He had told no one else.

We fully understood that if Ernie was to be helped by the specialist, he had to tell the truth. But if he told the truth, the doctor would think he was crazy. What was he to do? Since his mother had all ready heard him call out to Glory Rose in his sleep, she believed his depression had truly been the result of bad dreams.

We children decided that Ernie should tell the doctor about his "bad dream", the Domes, the royal pigs, the little people and everything. But he must never tell anyone else, not even his parents. He agreed.

Ernie's problem concerned us a great deal. However, it did not stop us from going to the cellar. The problems were all related. If we could solve The Queen's problem, we could somehow solve Ernie's.

With Mom's food basket in hand we returned to the cellar. A few seconds later Tackett arrived at the door, smiling.

"Good morning, friends, I have missed you." He looked at me. "You got my message."

I nodded. "Please tell us, is everything all right? How is Her Highness?"

"The Rose Queen begs your forgiveness and invites you to return with me, as soon as possible." His eyes were filled with hope as he looked to us for an answer. He noticed Ernie was not with us. "Wait, the smallest one is not yet here! Her Highness would be sorely disappointed if Ernie did not come along. He makes her laugh. She finds so little to be happy about these days, but the little fellow's honesty gives her great pleasure."

What a strange situation! Would Ernie ever see The Queen again?

Chapter 14. Center Stage

"Sorry to have to tell you the news, Tackett. Ernie has worried himself sick over The Queen. He is too ill to play in the cellar," Iva reported sadly. "Our parents have taken him to see a doctor and now he must go see a specialist. All we can do is hope that Queen Glory Rose finds good fortune, either by letting us plant the gardens or finding a replacement somehow for the magic."

"Or give birth to a new Queen!" I added. Was it too much to hope for?

"Oh! I have news also. Her Highness is expecting another litter of pigs," Tackett announced. His voice lacked the enthusiasm and joy that ordinarily accompanies such an proclamation. But Tackett had announced the news as if he were saying, "Tomorrow if we're lucky, the sun may shine". He had lost hope.

I was irritated at Tackett's attitude. In Missouri, we never gave up hope. When I heard news of another litter, I felt optimistic.

I said, "Oh yes!" I closed my eyes, crossed my fingers on both hands and wished hard. The Ellison kids followed suit.

Tackett did not understand us. He was getting antsy.

"Can you go with me, children?" he asked politely.

"Let's go," Billy smiled at the little man.

The Transit Basket had not lost its magic. We embarked joyfully, as if we had done it all our lives, absent of all fear.

Once again we were mesmerized by the scent of roses and the shower of lights. Then a bit of a tug of the magical basket told us we had arrived. But where was it we had arrived?

When the mist cleared permitting us to see through the spaces between the wicker, we discovered we were definitely not in The Queen's rose garden. This Dome looked like a small scale football stadium.

We had settled ourselves near a large stage located in the center of a bowl-like auditorium. Most of the surrounding seats were small of course to accommodate the elves. However, second story and center stage were large to larger pink seats, no doubt reserved for Her Royal Highness, Queen Glory Rose and her family or aides.

Bells began to chime. Lovely, deep sounds, resembling the chimes of a giant striking clock. Perhaps it **was** a striking clock, somewhere in The Dome.

Little people were pouring in to the auditorium by way of four hallways, one on each side of the building. Obviously, they anticipated an event about to take place. Merrily they bounced along, holding hands and talking cheerfully to each other.

So far, the stage was bare. Our only entertainment was the sound of the chimes, which had softened somewhat, but continued to ring.

Those who came wore dressy apparel. The standard pink on the men and green on the women, was noticeable. Except today, the fabric was light weight, rich brocades and lace, stylish indeed. Pretty hats adorned with fresh flowers sat atop the heads of the younger girls. Today, for the first time, I paid more attention to their footwear. Many of them wore turned up, pointed toed shoes, like the leprechauns.

Now the stage was being decorated with baskets of fresh flowers. Several very elegant looking white chairs with gold trim were brought in and placed together on the stage. Everyone smiled at us standing there by the Transit Basket.

A small band of musicians and a couple of dozen young men and women singers took their place on the stage. Then we were escorted up on the stage by several couples of little people. Tackett evidently knew what was going to happen, but he didn't tell us.

Once we were seated, the musicians struck up a slow but powerful rendition. Everyone stood up as if in great expectation.

Suddenly, a brilliant pink Transit Basket appeared. Its radiance illuminated the stage. And guess who it was.

Her Highness, the Rose Queen, looking every bit like a Queen, stepped gracefully from the magnificent vehicle, being assisted by her ever present young aides. She wore a full length, golden frock of soft velvet, topped by a very ornate, matching coverlet of lustrous satin. On her head was a jeweled crown.

Everyone had dropped to one knee and smiled lovingly at their Queen. Not wanting to appear impolite or ignorant, we followed suit.

While we bowed there, a thought crossed my mind. What would our parents and friends say, if they saw us bowing to a pig? I could see them laughing. But to us, she wasn't just any pig, she was a magical Queen. And, we had become more than fond of her.

The Rose Queen smiled at her subjects and motioned for them to be seated. The Dome became as silent as the shadows in anticipation of her address. It was perfectly clear, the elves adored their Queen.

We sat to the right of where she stood. She directed a friendly smile toward us and we smiled back.

"My dear friends," she said, then turning toward the main body of elves, she continued. "My loyal subjects. Thank you for answering my invitation. As always, in the past, I have shared with you my hopes, my dreams and my fears concerning our lives. Today, the most urgent problem faces us." The elves responded with faint sounds and expressive faces.

"Our young friends from another place may well hold the answer to our problem. They have just returned to us. I must speak with them before I address you. So, please sing

happy songs to cheer us all, while we talk. And wait, if you please, upon my return."

As she turned, the elves dropped again to one knee. A couple of The Queen's young aides walked toward us delivering an invitation to follow them into the Transit Basket. I wondered where we were going.

Her weight really rocked the basket. Billy giggled. Iva put a finger to her lips.

Tackett and the aides did not follow us into the Transit Basket. We seated ourselves comfortably around her. Straightaway, I noticed how much weight she had gained. After all, she was expecting!

I had never known that pink and gold went well together, referring of course to The Queen's gold clothing over her pink body. On her, the gold looked quite suitable.

It didn't appear we were going anyplace. This was to be a private place for us to talk.

"We are glad to see you," I told her.

"We were plenty worried!" Billy added.

"Did you really send for us?" Laura asked.

"Yes, I sent for you. I should have done it sooner. We need you now more than ever! Because of my stubbornness I have placed my kingdom in great danger! Can you help me, children? Are we too late? Tell me as quickly as you can. Can you teach us to grow our own food without magic?" she asked frantically. "And can we accomplish this great task soon enough to prevent my subjects and my family from perishing?"

Wow! A lot of questions for a bunch of kids!

"All it takes is good earth and seed!" Billy answered happily. "We are ready when you give the orders!"

"Does Billy speak for all of you? You can help us then?" she asked.

Iva assured the Rose Queen that we were of one mind and how we had thought of nothing else since we left her. Iva explained that seed was available to us. Available because we lived in a town where people were very giving, and cared about each other. If someone was in need, our Watson community, out of kindness, quickly stepped up to help.

"Tell me, Your Highness, how do you grow so many beautiful roses and bushes and stuff, without soil?" I asked curiously.

"Pure magic, my friend, pure wonderful magic," she smiled at me.

"Well then, if you can grow roses magically, then why can't you grow vegetables?" Laura had made a good point. Why did she need us?

Chapter 15. Telling the Elves

For a moment The Queen looked quite sad. "Oh children, I have not tricked you. Yes, we are allowed to grow our flowers by magic. We live under rules put into place many, many years ago. The growth of our flowers comes about by touching a Thistledown Orb, like the one you've seen on Tackett's hat. Oddly enough, the magic of the little Orb does not work on producing food. The Primer Pot is our only means of getting food and the Primer Pot, like the Orb has limited powers."

"We don't believe you tricked us, Your Highness. We didn't understand how your magic works! Did we kids?" I wanted to reassure her.

"Boy! My Mama loves roses," Laura laughed. "Would she ever like to have some of that magic!"

Laura's good humor caused The Queen to think of Ernie.

"And where is the funny little chap? Why is he not with you?"

We were hesitant to tell The Queen that she was the cause of Ernie's illness. No one wanted to hurt her feelings. After all we were visitors in a strange land. The local folks might not take too kindly to us accusing their Queen. One of us had to tell her something! Each of us waited upon the other to do it. Finally, Billy blurted out the answer.

"Ernie is at home sick."

"Sick?" The Queen exclaimed. "How sick?"

"Too sick to come with us." Laura searched our faces to see if we approved of her answer. Seeing no frowns or the shaking of heads, she went a step farther.

"He is worried about you, Your Highness. Ernie really took a liking to you. We promised him we'd come back here, if you sent for us, and do what we could to help you. I know when we tell him you've changed your mind about uncovering some soil, he'll feel much better."

Glory Rose groaned at the thought of exposing "dirt". But she was dismayed that Ernie's illness was her fault. She confessed to us she felt guilty indeed.

Billy giggled when The Queen groaned about exposing dirt. He figured she could not help the way she felt.

The Queen spoke to her aids waiting outside. "I am ready now to make the announcement." And to us she said, "Come with me, please."

Once the Rose Queen stepped out on the stage, the music rang to a spirited climax, and those who waited upon her arrival, dropped to one knee.

We seated ourselves back on the stage.

Glory Rose strode to center stage, assisted by those lovely pastel, teenage looking, aides, the same ones who had attended her in the palace.

An elegant white column rose up from the floor where she stood. I assumed it was for leaning, as it was the height for doing so. I was correct.

The Dome people bowed from the waist until The Queen invited them to be seated. Before they sat they shouted a greeting.

"Hail great Queen, heir of magic. Good health. Long life. We pledge thee our honor. Hail to thee!"

After having paid her homage, they quietly took their seats. Loving, smiling faces awaited her message.

A small circle of stage where The Queen and the column stood, raised slightly, and then revolved very slowly. Rotating, as she did, she was able to face all of them in the bowl shaped auditorium an equal amount of time. What a clever idea!

Standing on hind legs, as always, regal and erect, Her Highness stood at least seven feet tall, maybe more.

"My dear loyal friends," she began. "The time has come for me to face the serious situation lying ahead of us. I am growing old. Even though the Ancient Elders have written by decree, foretelling that each Rose Queen will give birth to a replacement, one who possesses the keys to magic upon which we live, that event has not come to pass. My common sense commands. All magic may leave The Domes when I depart this life."

Some of the elves moaned and cried! "No, no, dear Queen, you must never leave us." Another sobbed, "Whatever shall we do, Your Highness?" And another, "What will become of us?"

Their words tore at The Queen's heart. She was greatly saddened for she loved the elves and knew they depended upon her for their very lives. She felt she had failed them as no other Queen before her had. But she was willing to sacrifice and to make changes. The changes were extremely hard for her. She then nodded toward us, seated there near her.

"You have met our visitors, children from another place. Our magic is new and exciting to them. In their land, food is grown in the ground, from soil. We call it dirt. My royal family is so fanatically clean, no dirt or soil is allowed exposed. Carpet covers every patch. But now we must learn from the children. We must grow food, as if there were no magic. If we do not do this, my friends, you will surely starve to death."

The Queen had made us the center of attention. The elves were gawking at us and we were about as uncomfortable as a grasshopper in the hen house. But we felt important knowing we were needed.

"The children will tell us what to do and we will do it. They will be our teachers and we will learn. We must learn to live without magic."

Again there were groans. Poor things, they didn't know how much fun gardening is!

"Tackett will choose a few of you to meet with him and the children. Be quick about it and do exactly as the children instruct you. Your survival may depend upon it." Now The Queen wept unashamedly. Seeing her anguish, those loving young assistants hurried to her side to attend to her return to the Transit Basket.

Again, her subjects bowed as she departed from the stage. Many of them wiped tears from their eyes. I felt sure most of them did not truly understand the urgency of her message. I believe they were sad merely because their Rose Queen was sad.

Tackett stood, raised his hands for the elves to listen, and made a brief statement. "Be watching for a drop of news. I shall keep you all informed."

A drop of news? What in the world was a drop of news?

The elves left the Dome with a lot less hoopla than they had entered. Now that The Queen had spoken, Tackett was sure he could depend upon them.

It was an urgent matter. We told Tackett how to begin. As soon as we could locate plots for planting and get them uncovered, the spading could proceed. Then, we would go get seed and the planting could begin.

"What if the soil is no good?" I asked. "Then what do we do? We can't bring soil!"

"Isn't all soil the same?" Laura inquired innocently.

"No way. I read up on it. Daddy gave me these books to read. I learned a lot," I told her. "Maybe there will be worms."

"Dweeds?" Tackett laughed. "Those things are everywhere!"

"I don't think so. Are they earthworms?" I probed.

"Earthworms?" Tackett did not understand.

"You know, worms that live in the soil!" I informed the elf.

"Aren't you forgetting something? Our soil is carpeted. How could the dweeds get through it?"

I laughed. "Sorry, I forgot!"

Next, we flew around The Domes in the Aero Gobbetts looking for garden spots, locating several. Finally, we settled on three centrally located areas.

Our instructions to Tackett were simple. Remove the carpeting and spade up the ground.

"What is a spade?" Tackett asked us.

Iva tried to describe one. The elf handed her a piece of paper and a little sharp stick.

"Here, draw a picture of one," he suggested.

Iva passed the paper to Billy, who drew very well. In a couple of minutes Billy showed Tackett what a spade looked like.

The elf used the same magic Ernie used in the Deli-Dome when he could not spell "Strawberry Sundae" for the Primer Pot. He closed his eyes, stomped his right foot and before him, on the carpet were five perfectly good shovels, exactly the size for an elf.

Then we learned what a "drop of news" was. Tackett prepared a message, asking for several men to show up at the three addresses where garden spots would be prepared. The message was reproduced by a touch of what we had learned from Tackett to be the Thistledown Orb on his hat. After making lots of copies he flew around, "dropping the news" from the Aero Gobbett. The leaflets floated down to anxious, uplifted hands.

Straightaway, the little people headed for the gardens spots. Soon the carpeting was removed. Some of them held their noses as if the dirt smelled bad. Perhaps it did.

More shovels were produced. We gave them demonstrations on how to use a shovel. The spading would take a little longer, even though there were eight or nine men at each location.

The soil was dry and sick looking, but the men learned how to turn it, in nothing flat. They sang as they shoveled.

Tackett took us home to gather up seed. Our plan was to collect all the seed, plants and onion sets we could carry. While we girls scavenged Watson, Billy went home to check on Ernie.

Billy found Ernie huddled in the big rope hammock in their back yard. He was no better ---perhaps even more withdrawn.

Billy sank down to his knees by his brother. Ernie was pale. His fairness gave the black circles around his eyes an even more sickening look.

"Hey, Ernie! How ya doin', buddy?" Billy tried being cheerful for his brother's sake. Glancing around to make sure they were alone, Billy told his Ernie the good news.

"It's gonna be all right, Ernie. We have just come from The Domes. We've been with Glory Rose today. She has changed her mind. Right now the elves are taking up the carpeting and are spading up the ground. We are going back tomorrow with seed! You'll see, everything's gonna be o.k."

Ernie looked straight into his brother's eyes, hoping for the right news. "Has The Queen had a magic baby yet?" He whispered weakly.

"No she hasn't, but don't you see, they are gonna grow their own food, just like we do. Don't worry! We'll make expert gardeners out of those little people," he smiled at his brother. It was no use. Ernie wanted to hear only one thing. And that was, The Queen had given birth to a new Rose Queen. The boy was wasting away.

In no time at all we were loaded down with seed packets, plants and onion sets. We sneaked them into the cellar when no one was looking and hid them under the potato bins.

Telling the Elves

Billy gave us a full report on Ernie. It wasn't good.

"We've got another problem," I told Billy. "Daddy wants you and me to help him repair fence tomorrow. How can we refuse? If we beg out he will know something is wrong. We have never ever in all our lives refused to help Daddy when he needed us. Iva and Laura will have to go without us with Tackett to take the stuff to The Domes."

The girls looked at each other. Going by themselves was a little scary. But there was no other way.

Billy and I met Daddy at 8:00 a.m., after chores. In preparation we had hitched our small Farmall tracter to a wagon, loaded the wagon with fencing tools and were ready when Daddy got there. Billy even filled a water jug from our well in the back yard. The sooner we got to the job and got it finished, the better.

No matter how we tried, our thoughts were with Iva and Laura. Would they be all right, alone?

Chapter 16. Peculiar Gardening and Peculiar Clouds

Daddy was pleased with us for getting everything ready to do the fencing. He pointed the way. Billy drove the tractor, and loved it. Daddy and I sat in the back of the wagon and let our feet dangle.

Nicky, our old Collie-Shepherd stock dog, ran along behind.

George and Elsie Ellison had caught the train to Kansas City long before sunup, taking Ernie to the specialist.

We were positive Iva and Laura were in The Domes by this time with their big basket full of seeds. Even though they were a little spooked, they could handle it.

When we came to the house for our noon meal my mother was coming in from the cellar. I caught my breath. Did she see anything? Or suspect anything? I hurried to the kitchen and saw her set down a quart of peaches and a small jar of sweet pickles.

"Are you hungry?" she smiled.

"Yes," I answered. All was well. She had gone down for food.

Quickly, we washed up and enjoyed Mama's cooking. In those days in Missouri, we called lunch "dinner", and dinner was supper. The big meal was served at noon, unless there was company. In that case Mama piled the table high every time we ate.

There was ham-hock and navy beans. I skipped the ham-hocks. We also had greens, sliced tomatoes, sweet pickles and corn bread. For dessert we had sliced peaches and sugar cookies.

"Colene, I found your note in the cellar."

Billy almost choked on his food.

"It was a nice note," Mama said, "and very thoughtful."

"What did it say?" my dad was curious.

Billy was about to have a hissy fit. I had left a note for my family the day before, just in case we did not return. But I gave away no secrets.

"The note just said she loved her family," Mama told Daddy.

Billy looked at me and wiped his brow.

Daddy smiled, "That was nice, honey. We love you too."

Mama wanted to know how the fencing was going.

"Great!" Daddy reported. "You'll never find two kids who can outwork these two. We repaired all the pasture fencing, the busted gate where the bull broke through and part of the corn field fencing. I'll turn hogs in there this fall to pick up what we leave in the harvesting. We'll spend a couple more hours tightening the fence there and that ought to do it."

"Them ol' hogs will be too busy hogging down that corn to get out, Harry," Billy

announced.

Daddy laughed. "I hope you're right, son. I never did enjoy chasing hogs."

"Billy, your mama told me that she and your daddy were going to take Ernie to a Shirley Temple show in Kansas City. It might cheer him up," Mama said.

"It will take a real funny movie to get him to laugh," Billy said thoughtfully.

"Poor little fellow. George said he's wasting away, lost about twelve pounds. Quite a lot for a boy!" my daddy said. Daddy was very tender hearted. My parents loved all the Ellisons.

"Ernie could sure use some good news," I said.

My mom agreed, but only Billy understood what I meant.

Although we worked hard and fast on the fencing, the hours dragged. Keeping my mind off the girls was impossible.

Two little girls working hard at teaching gardening to a kingdom of elves, governed by a pig who walked upright, talked, wore clothes, a kingdom that was squeaky clean and provided food for everybody by tossing a piece of paper in a pot. Were we nuts, or not? Who would believe it? Nobody! That's why we had to keep our mouths shut and that was what was killing Ernie. What would become of us? I tried not to think about it.

George and Elsie were not expected home with Ernie until quite late, probably on the ten o'clock train. Maybe that's why Iva and Laura were not back yet. They knew they had time. But when dusk came, I began to worry.

About 8:30 Billy and I told my folks we were going to the cellar to tell ghost stories and eat apples. We hurried down to wait it out. The girls arrived about 9:00 p.m., tired and hungry.

"Those little people are like nobody else!" Iva laughed. "They spaded. They threw dirt clods at each other! They laughed and sang and seemed to fool around half the time, but there were so many who were willing to help, the work got done."

Billy and I were sorry we had missed out on all the fun.

"The soil looked sick," Laura reported. " I don't know whether it will grow anything or not! It was dry and dusty. The little plot was surrounded by pigs. I swear, they tried to destroy the dust before it settled. They were really funny and worked harder than anybody."

"But we did get everything planted. They learned fast, those elves. And, when one learned, that one taught someone else. It worked out great! Except, they wanted to eat the onion sets instead of planting them and every time we stirred up a little dust, someone would say, 'Oh, I hope our dear Queen doesn't see this' ", Iva said.

Laura began to laugh. "The funniest thing was the rain shower. Iva told them the garden needed a good shower of rain, so someone rubbed a Thistledown Orb. Guess what? A little rain cloud formed over the garden and gave it a good soaking. We nearly laughed our heads off. Of course they all laughed at us."

"You left out part of the story, Laura," Iva grinned. "You gotta hear this. Tackett asked if anybody knew what a rain cloud was. I had told him that in Missouri we let the rain clouds water the garden most of the time. An old lady put up her hand."

"I do, I know what **a rain crowd** is! My Lootie fed one to me when I was a smaller person." The old woman was just being silly and having fun. Everybody laughed at her.

"I had to draw a picture of a rain cloud so they could come up with one. I needed Billy to do a better drawing, but since he wasn't there, my picture had to do."

"Even the soil looked fake, as well as looking sick. I'm too tired to think about whether the seed will sprout or not." Laura yawned. She had worked hard and was tired.

There was more to tell.

Iva told us about the dweeds. Those crazy dweeds, as she put it. As soon as the soil was exposed the dweeds came around. Surprisingly enough, they wanted to help. They watched when the girls set a stake at the end of the row with a seed packet turned upside down, to show what was planted there. They caught on fast. After the packet was put up, they made their own sign by crawling out the letters, laying down some kind of green ooze from their bodies. Iva said it was sickening to her and Laura, but the elves thought it was funny. The elves were used to them.

"I can't wait to see what all you did with the gardens. And another thing, I want to see outside The Domes. What is out there? Where are they located? Where are the Ancient Elders The Queen talks about? Who are those guys? I'd sure feel a lot better if I had the answers to a few questions. Wouldn't you?"

Iva agreed with me. "Me too! I'm ready to see more. Tackett will be here day after tomorrow at 9:00 a.m."

It wasn't just me. We were all eager to get back to The Domes.

My mother called to us from the kitchen porch.

"Kids, I am going across the street to see how Ernie is. I just saw their lights go on." We all flew up the stairs.

"We'll go too," Billy hollered. "Mom will want us home now anyway."

"You kids are going to turn into frogs if you don't stay out of that dark cellar! Every other kid in town is tan from the sun. But this bunch looks like the dead of winter," she scowled at us.

"But Hattie," Laura teased, "Other kids don't have a great cellar to play in like we do."

"Lord knows you must love it, you're down there enough," Mama said as we headed across the road to Ellison's house. "At least I always know where you are. Don't you ever get bored?"

Poor Mom, if she only knew. We all began to laugh. We had been to places and seen things too unbelievable to share, even with her. Billy really snickered.

Elsie was getting a half-sleeping Ernie into his pajamas.

"Would one of you girls run over to Sharps and get Beverly? Hilda took care of her today for me." Elsie handed Ernie to his dad who carried him in to bed.

"What did the doctor say about him, Elsie?" Mama asked.

Elsie was worn out. She dropped down on the couch.

"He's a puzzle, Hattie. The doctor thinks it all has to do with his bad dreams. Now can you get this. Ernie told the doctor, but he didn't want us to know anything about it! But he talks in his sleep. Maybe Ernie thinks we'll worry if we know. It's not a girl named Glory Rose, now it's a pig and a talking pig at that."

Oh, no! Ernie would keep on talking in his sleep and tell them everything. What if they made us stay out of the cellar?

Chapter 17. Back to The Domes

"None of it makes any sense," Elsie worried. "Maybe we should keep him awake so he won't dream. We're supposed to keep him busy, keep his mind off the dream. Reading to him will help. You kids will have to relieve me once in a while. He does like to be read to. Keep him out of the cellar! He needs fresh air and exercise."

"Out of the cellar?" Billy bellowed. "What's the matter with the cellar? Ernie likes that place! It's his favorite place to play! You said you wanted us to read to him. We read and tell stories in the cellar all the time!"

"But Billy, your mother is right! You kids are white as ghosts from spending so much time down in that old musty cellar. And maybe its all those scary stories you kids tell that's got Ernie so afraid!" my mother added. "There are lots of other good places to play, all over the farm. Even the barn loft lets in light. You kids used to play up there a lot."

Iva and I slipped silently into the kitchen. Were we responsible for Ernie's condition? Probably. I felt like crying. Somehow, we had to work our own kind of magic in The Domes. The way we figured it, growing their own food will keep the Dome residents going. So what if they didn't have the magic of the Aero Gobbetts and the Transit Basket. They could walk. The community of The Domes was not really that large. In fact, it was no bigger than Watson and we walked all over town.

Iva and I were committed to doing anything we had to do, to help Ernie get well.

Billy ran upstairs to check on Ernie. Good! He was asleep! Billy looked down at his brother.

"Don't talk in your sleep, Ernie," he said softly. "You're getting us all in trouble."

From that day on, two of us remained with Ernie, and two went to The Domes.

I was glad when Laura and Billy volunteered to stay with Ernie the next day.

Mama and I headed back across the street to our house. She was more worried about Ernie than she had let on to Elsie. I heard her tell Daddy that George and Elsie planned to take turns sitting up with Ernie in case he talked in his sleep. And he was sure to do that, a fact that worried us kids greatly.

Laura planned to tell her little brother everything that happened in the gardens with the elves and dweeds. Surely, it would cheer him up. But, who could tell, maybe not!

An open door awaited Iva and me in the cellar the next morning, but what was this? Tackett was not there! We raced down the hallway to see if the Transit Basket was there. It was. But still no sign of our guide.

"What do you make of this?" I asked my friend.

"Beats me!"

Then another wonder occurred! As we stood there gawking at that pink wicker pig,

its door opened. An invitation? Of course. We had come to expect anything. So, why not? We stepped into the coach and sat down. Somehow, the little basket worked its magic, even without Tackett there to touch the little Thistledown Orb. As quickly as ever, we had reached our destination.

The rose garden, exquisite and unchanged, lay before us. Once again, Handel greeted us, and bid us welcome to the Royal gardens and to the palace.

Without delay, The Queen's ever helpful young attendants took us to where she lay lounging on a large couch of sorts. This one had a super soft cushion into which The Queen had settled comfortably. The head of the couch was much higher than the foot.

Iva and I bowed respectfully and clumsily to The Queen who laughed and told us as she always did, it wasn't necessary. She had gained a lot of weight. The due date of her expected litter must surely be near.

"How are you feeling, Your Majesty?" I asked, truly concerned about this secret friend of ours.

"When food is being harvested from the gardens, I will feel much better," she smiled. "I thank you, my young friends, with all my heart for coming to our rescue. Imagine, three large gardens planted already. Growing food is something we never counted on! A new way of life, but necessary if we are to survive now and long after I have passed from this life."

Our visit lasted the better part of an hour. We learned a lot. These pigs lived for about 30 years. The Rose Queens had always given birth to the succeeding Queens anywhere from their 22nd year to their 25th year. The new heir was born a Princess. She became Queen only after the death of the mother Queen. Queen Glory Rose had been in her 26th year for over six months. Never before had a Rose Queen given birth after her 25th year. No more babies and certainly not a Rose Queen heir.

"I have angered the Ancient Elders, but how or when is a mystery to me. It is they who select and teach the new heir before she is born. Only after she has mastered the teachings of the wise ones will she be given to us. But we have been passed over. What has happened to them? Have they forgotten me? Or, perhaps, they themselves cease to exist!" A tear made its way down her long cheek. Quickly, she changed the subject.

"Tackett is guarding the gardens and was unable to meet you today. The elves have a lot to learn. Because they get food from the Primer Pot, immediately, the little people thought all they had to do was put the seed in the ground, dig it up the next minute and find food." She laughed loudly, thinking about it. "They keep showing up with those new shovels, digging up the garden and finding nothing but seed, leaving them quite confused. Finally, Tackett had leaflets made up and did a drop of news. My little kingdom and their Queen must be educated on the time it takes for food to grow in the ground."

"The little people worked hard getting the gardens spaded and the seed planted. They are so happy and they love you so much, Your Majesty," Iva tried to console The Queen.

"And to think, I will be The Queen to let them down." Her voice trailed off pitifully.

"Well it ain't over until it's over!" I piped up.

Giving me the strangest look, she replied, "But don't you see, Colene, it is over. I have passed the age to bear a Rose Queen!"

More than anything, I longed to give her hope, "Perhaps you haven't, after all."

We shrank from talking about Ernie and his illness. But somehow, we had a feeling she knew.

Given use of the Royal Gobbetts, pink ones of course instead of silver like the others, we meandered through The Domes. Friendly greetings drifted up to us from the elves. We waved and smiled down at them.

Soon, we spotted Tackett and his helpers, keeping a lookout for elves with shovels. The elves meant well. They just didn't know any better.

By the end of three days seed would be sprouting and a few green leaves would show through the soil. In a week, almost everything should be up. At least that is the way it happened in Missouri.

But Laura had been right. The soil did look dead. Too bad we couldn't bring soil too! If this dead soil wouldn't produce food, then what were we to do?

Chapter 18. Love Those Dweeds

By the time we reached the Deli-Dome, lunch time was fast approaching. The Primer Pot lids bumped and banged and the smell of the food tantalized us.

Oddly enough, we forgot the lure of the food when a new and curious incident caught our eyes.

Taking away the food scraps and refuse was a cute little tanker truck, a peculiar looking, blimp shaped rig that rolled along on three rows of black balls, instead of tires. Of course it was immaculately white! No sign of garbage hung over or squeezed out like the ones we had seen in the cities in Missouri.

We were curious. Where did they take it? Where would The Queen permit them to dump it? That particular, squeaky clean, Queen!

A good excuse to snoop. We followed the funny looking little vehicle. Moving rather slowly, it turned down a carpeted street, heading toward an exit. This exit was the only one covered by a solid door.

There were two elves in the truck. As soon as they spotted us trailing along behind them, they began to laugh and bounce up and down.

In order to speak to them we had to lower our Aero Gobbett and move along beside them. Apparently, no one had ever shown interest in their job. I suppose that explains their surprise when we told them we wanted to see where they dumped their garbage. The funny little men laughed so hard we thought they might burst. They motioned for us to follow. The big solid door opened automatically. Our Aero Gobbett nearly dragged on the carpet as we passed through the door behind the garbage truck.

Once outside that door, we were really outside, you know, sky and everything. However, the sky was a pinkish gold and there were two small suns. At least, we thought they were suns. Looking directly at them, our eyes did not water, even though they gave off plenty of light.

The little garbage truck passed by row after row of large containers. Open containers filled with what looked like soil. They were shaped like half a large football, measuring about eight feet long and five feet wide.

Then suddenly, there they were. Dweeds! Hundreds of them, hanging all over the receptacles.

This then was the dumping place. The men stopped, stepping out on rich green grass, or was it carpet? They chose several partially filled containers, dumping some of their load in each of them.

The dweeds attacked the garbage, some from the top and some from the sides. They burrowed deep, wiggling their tails until we could no longer see them.

I wanted to see it for myself, up close. We found only one place to park the Aero Gobbett. The elves, still smiling broad smiles came to where we had parked.

I had to feel of that soil in the containers. Iva thought I was crazy. But I remembered what I had read.

"This stuff is worm castings, Iva. Daddy let me read a book about it. There is no soil richer than this. It's like gold. The Queen has a gold mine here." The elves watched closely. "I wish I had some seed! I'd plant it out here, right now!

One of the little men crossed his feet where he stood, and an ample smile showed a mouthful of white but pointed teeth, "My name is Clocko. What kind of seed you want, Missy?"

"I don't care, Clocko, what kind ya got?" I smiled back.

"Clocko helped put seed in dirt yesterday. I know what seed look like. You tell Clocko what you want and I will go to the Orb. Orb get you seed." He told us.

"If the Orb can give you seed, then why did we tramp all over Watson from house to house collecting it for you?" Iva was a little aggravated.

I agreed with Iva. "O.K. Clocko, give me a handful of green bean seed."

Grinning, the elf touched the Orb on his hat and held out an empty hand to me, still grinning up at me.

"So, where's the seed?" Iva asked.

Clocko looked down at his hand. His smile turned slowly to surprise. The other elf grabbed Clocko's hand and looked. They could not believe the Orb had failed them. The men did not understand. But I did. Seeds were food, or at least they turned into to edible objects and food came only from the Primer Pots. The Queen said so herself. I explained it to the elves, offering comfort for their disappointment. After all, they were trying to be helpful.

"Wait! I just remembered something," Iva said anxiously. She put her hand in her deep pinafore pocket and pulled out a modest number of seeds, along with a ribbon from her doll's hair and a bubble gum wrapper.

"Here," she showed us. "To heck with the Orb, this is the real stuff, left over from yesterday!" she teased.

There were about a dozen seeds in all, radishes, beets, lettuce and green beans. So, we had green bean seed after all. We scouted out the best looking soil and planted the seed.

"Please, please, don't eat the seed!" Iva pleaded with the dweeds. The funny little characters gawked straight at her, making faces.

The soil smelled wonderful. I asked how they kept it so nice out here. After all, they had green grass, sky and good soil. I wondered why the pigs and elves didn't come outside more. Maybe they did when we aren't around.

The second elf, known as Bleekers, told me how they did it.

"We load old dirty dirt from over the hill. Bring back and stick on top of food junk, keep from stinking!" He held his belly and chuckled a screechy laugh. "That dirty dirt plugs up noses on Clocko and Bleekers so not get wrinkles from bad stink. Whoo, yeah!"
He fanned the air in front of his nose and cackled some more. "Dweeds chew and spit dirt all day long!"

The grass underfoot was truly grass and according to Bleeker it never changed. It never died out. In fact, neither of the men knew what dying out meant. Apparently, the grass always remained the same height, never grew taller, never had to be trimmed. Strange.

For some reason, when beams of lights encircled the garbage truck, sanitizing it before it re-entered the Deli-Dome, we were not surprised.

Iva and I followed along behind in our Aero Gobbett, but we did not get sanitized. Why not, we wondered?

When I looked at Iva, I had to laugh. A dweed with the tiny head of a small boy, had wrapped himself around Iva's ear.

"Come down from there!" she demanded. "You are disturbing my pleasant morning. If I wanted something on my ear, I would not choose a worm."

The dweed leaped to the top of her head and spit green slime on her nose. Iva seemed ready to kill that worm.

I knew it wasn't nice, but I had to laugh, "The nasty thing," I said. The dweed turned his attention to me. How he did it, I don't know. But he spat a powerful gob of that same green gunk and it landed squarely on my face.

Now it was Iva laughing. "Maybe we had better back up and get sanitized," she snickered. We did it, and it turned out to be the most fun we had all day. No water, just beams of light to clean us. Afterwards, there was no sign of the dweed. Thank goodness!

Our next stop was the garden where Tackett kept watch. Of all the elves we had encountered, Tackett was the best educated. One day I would ask him about it.

I told him about the garbage pits and the great soil. Although he appeared interested, he had no idea what I was talking about. Maybe it was the thought of eating food grown in garbage and worm castings. It does sound gross, but the end result is short of a miracle. Magic perhaps. Magic they understood and might accept.

The Queen had directed Tackett to show their fitness center to us, of which she was very proud. Following her wishes, he directed our attention to the Dome housing their hospitals, doctors offices and other health care buildings.

First, we would eat. Since we had none of my mother's food today, we proposed to eat with the locals.

Again the elves made us feel like celebrities while they crowded around to greet us and stared at what we were eating.

Iva and I both ordered what every other kid in Missouri ordered, cheeseburgers, french fries and a coke. But the Primer Pot would not give us cheeseburgers. Why? Because they contain meat! O.K. So, we'd try again. This time we ordered chef salads and lemonade. Bingo. Everyone watched the pots. Out come two great looking chef salads lacking the usual ham and beef strips. Even without the meat, they were great.

Without thinking, I asked Iva if she missed the ham and beef from her salad. Several elves standing by gazed long and steadily at us. Tackett put his finger to his lips to quiet us. What had we done? Did the elves understand that ham and beef were meat? Meat that we eat? I hoped not!

Chapter 19. Home

Our faithful little guide explained to us about the elves. They only knew the Primer Pots would not produce anything unkind to our bodies. Evidently, we had them all curious about our rejected order. I hoped they never found out about Missourians eating a lot of ham.

Many of the elves liked the looks of our salads. Within a few minutes, everybody around us was trying chef salads and lemonade. They loved the salad, but they spit the lemonade all over themselves and each other trying to get rid of it. Life with them was a constant party. They laughed about everything.

We heard music from the time we entered the Deli-Dome. It came from a group roaming around the street tables. Now, they came to us and drew a crowd. We smiled and ate and let our feet keep time with the music. How kind and loving they were. We had grown very fond of them. Many were becoming quite familiar to us.

An unexpected troupe of acrobats came tumbling down the street doing cartwheels, one after the other. Before us were about a dozen young gymnasts really showing off. They were good! They jumped so high to be so short. Piling up on each other's shoulders, it took three of them to be as tall as my dad. But they piled higher and higher. More than half of them were boys. They were dressed in black gym clothes and red leprechaun type shoes. I was surprised to see those colors. Nowhere had we seen anything except pastels. After the group entertained us with their very professional stunts, the musicians played and they began dancing equally as well as they performed gymnastics.

We finally had to move on.

I had wondered about white pigs. Apparently, if you were born white you were destined to become involved in health care.

This health care Dome was gorgeous. The building were constructed of white boards and crystal blocks. The only color present was a pale blue, blue carpet, inside and out, blue curtains and blue trimming here and there.

The doctors, nurses and others giving care were all white pigs.

It was evident the care was for the royal family of pigs, including every pig on the place, as well as all the elves.

One of those light beam sanitizing gizmos was built into the entry of each building. I was impressed.

We were invited to inspect and explore the entire facility. Each time we went through another door we got zapped with the sanitizer. Talk about feeling squeaky clean! We did!

The doctors and nurses wore white jumpsuits and long white jackets.

Not being used to it, several elves affected by the dust from the gardens where

brought in for treatment.

Iva asked a nurse if they practice medicine or magic.

"That's a fair question," she answered. "When our medical knowledge fails we rely on magic. We never lose a patient. No one dies here except from old age."

The nurse was very intelligent. But I believe the Rose Queen was the most brilliant of them all.

The time had come for us to return home. Our day had been more than fruitful.

From The Queen's rose garden we sent a message telling her we would return in six days. We left word to keep the seed beds moist, but not wet and hoped they knew the difference.

Tackett bid us goodbye at the Transit Basket and we were again on our own.

Laura and Billy were in my back yard, waiting. Laura was slowly pushing Ernie in the big swing in the black walnut tree. Finding ourselves alone we delivered our report of the day's events.

Daddy should be told about those big containers full of worm castings. But I couldn't tell him.

Ernie was pleased to hear about the gardens. He even laughed about the stubborn Primer Pot for not serving up meat. He actually laughed out loud when he heard about the dweed around Iva's ear which spit green on us. What Ernie wanted to hear most of all, we were not able to tell him, for it was not true. "No, The Queen has not given birth to a special heir."

"But Ernie, she doesn't have babies every day. Maybe one will be born in this new batch of pigs she's expecting," Laura said.

"No, there won't be one and the magic will die with old Glory Rose." When he spoke, all hope drained from his face.

Nothing we could say made him smile again. Iva and I put our heads together. Maybe one day we might have to lie! Make up a story! Tell him an heir had been born. Anything, to make Ernie well.

The Ellison kids headed home. I picked up the milk buckets from the back porch. Mama heard me and came to have a look.

"I haven't seen you and Iva all day, but the other kids were here playing in the yard. Where have you been?" She wasn't mad at me, just curious.

"Oh, just pokin' around town," I answered. Of course, I neglected to tell her what town we were pokin' around in.

"Are you hungry?" she asked. That's the first thing she thought about. Mama didn't want anybody hungry.

"No, we had a vegetable salad with some friends," I answered honestly. I was not in the habit of lying to my parents.

I skee-daddled off the porch before she asked me any more questions.

Another thing that bothered me, I disliked having secrets from my mother.

Daddy had already let the cows into the milking barn and had them tied. He had something besides cows on his mind, I was sure. I went ahead doing the milking and singing, like always. Daddy watched me for a few moments, with a slight frown on his face, then turned and walked away.

The chores came and went. Daddy never did share with me what he was thinking.

Everybody in Watson was cooking and baking their special recipes for Ernie. He was the concern of the town. Elsie needed a lot of help to get him to eat. Ernie didn't lose any more weight, but he didn't gain back what he had lost either. The look Ernie wore on his face told us he was one troubled kid. The rest of us felt pretty guilty.

The next six days passed slowly. We had purposely stayed out of the cellar since my mother had chided us about looking so pale.

The night before we were to return to The Domes I sort of sidled up to Mama, buttering her up.

"Gosh Mom, have you noticed we haven't played in the cellar for a week? Are we tanner?"

Mom looked close at me. "Yes you are."

"I don't want to get too tan, nobody will recognize me. So I guess it's time we spend a day in the cellar," I grinned at her, trying my best to be tactful since I wanted something from her.

"Well I guess it won't hurt. And you kids have helped more than anyone else with Ernie. I'll talk to Elsie. I think it will be all right with her. I'll even pack a lunch," she offered. Good ol' Mom.

Yes, it was O.K. with Elsie. Except for Ernie, who had been taken over by the town, we'd all get to go to The Domes. Excitement set in, so much so that none of us slept much that night.

At nine o'clock sharp we headed for the Transit Basket. No one met us, but we managed to make the thing get us there. When we arrived in the rose garden, no one met us. How strange! And no one was working in the rose garden.

We stood there for a few minutes wondering what to do. Thank goodness, Tackett showed up in an Aero Gobbett.

He greeted us warmly but seemed most anxious to get back to the gardens, having guarded over them night and day since we planted the seed.

"The place looks deserted," Iva said to him, a little disturbed by it.

He did not answer.

We walked around to the side of the palace where the royal Aero Gobbetts were always parked. They were all gone.

Something is wrong, I could feel it! Tackett murmured something about the royal family cleaning the Aero Gobbetts often. Knowing how squeaky clean they were, I figured he was right. They were out for cleaning. Outside the quiet palace grounds, there were enough silver Aero Gobbetts for our use. He led the way.

Tackett had been bogged down with all the extra responsibility given to him by The Queen. He wanted to get back to the gardens as soon as possible. For that reason, he was not being very observant.

But I wanted to know. Where was everybody? What was going on?

Chapter 20. The Gardens

Tackett insisted we go immediately to the gardens. So we followed along reluctantly, in the Aero Gobbetts.

He said our first stop would be garden number one, the largest of the plots. Almost everything should to be through the ground at least in six days, radishes, lettuce, beans etc.

"Where is everybody?" I wondered, as we passed through the Deli-Dome and on into the residential Dome where the large plot was located.

"Well, how does it look?" Tackett was asking.

"Oh my goodness!" Billy frowned. "What happened?"

We parked near the garden.

The poor little elf looked worried! "Is it bad?"

"It isn't good," I answered. The leaves sticking their heads through the ground should have been healthy shades of green. But these were sickly looking, yellowish to pale green, showing signs of very poor soil. A good application of fertilizer if we had some, might be helpful. That's what my daddy would say.

"Let's go see if the other gardens look any better," Iva suggested.

Neither of them did. In fact, one looked much worse. I had never seen such a puny excuse for a garden in my life.

We were disappointed. I wanted to lie down and cry. They wouldn't eat meat, and we couldn't even give them vegetables!

How could we possibly break the news to The Queen?

Iva and I were eager to see what had happened to the seed we planted in the garbage dumps. I looked at her. She looked at me. I held my right hand close to my chest and flicked a pointing finger in the direction of the dumps.

"Let's go," she responded. "O.K. everybody, Colene and I are going outside to check on something. If you want to go with us, come on."

Laura and Billy had never been outside, so they were excited about going.

Tackett was startled. "Outside? There is nothing out there but worms and dumping vats." The elf deemed it to be a waste of time and he wasn't anxious to leave the gardens unguarded, but he watched as Iva and I headed in that direction. We Missourians are stubborn. When we make up our minds to do something, we do it.

"Delegate." I hollered to Tackett. The way he looked at me I guessed he did not know what "delegate" meant. "Ask someone else to watch the gardens for a few minutes. Anyone would be honored to work for you and The Queen." The thought had never occurred to him. Problem was, there was no one to ask. The crowd that always hung around us, was not there.

"Come on," Billy laughed. "Everybody's left town. So who's gonna bother the gardens?"

"Billy's right! This will only take a few minutes!" I begged.

Reluctantly, he left his post and headed out with us to the Deli-Dome. We learned something. If you were in a hurry, so were the Aero Gobbetts. They could really move. Iva and I were eager to see what happened to our seed planted in the worm castings.

Once through the big solid door and outside, Laura and Billy were too busy looking at the two suns and green grass to be interested in our seed. I parked my Aero Gobbett in the one parking place. The others had to hover next to the ground.

The search did not take long. We were overwhelmed by what we saw. The seed had produced fantastic results!

The green bean plants were over two inches tall. The leaves were broad, dark green and lush, extremely healthy looking. The radishes, lettuce and beets, all up, looked wonderful.

"Why?" Tackett asked. "I don't understand it at all. Seeds planted in garbage did better than those planted in the ground? And why didn't the dweeds eat them?"

"But Tackett, don't you see? It isn't garbage anymore!" I was as pleased as I had ever been, in my entire ten years. "Worms eat garbage and decayed stuff and turn it into soil. I read about it in one of my Daddy's books. No one need be hungry here, Tackett. If you lose your magic we have found another kind of magic for you in this good soil."

"The Queen must be told at once," Tackett always said that when there was news; he thought first of his Queen.

Going back through the door we were zapped by the sanitizer. Billy loved it.

"Can I take it home with me?" he smiled. "Mom could keep us kids all clean and we wouldn't even have to take a bath!"

I wondered where the dweeds were. Maybe they were underground. Not one was in sight.

Back in the Deli-Dome it was Tackett who finally realized how quiet it was, and noticed the absence of people. He had been so busy with the gardens and probably so tired that he had not missed them.

"Something is wrong! We must get to the palace quickly!" he cried, and peeled out, as a Missourian would say. We "peeled out" too, right behind him. Billy loved it.

As we reached the front gate of the palace we saw some pigs from the health care center entering. It looked like a doctor and two nurses.

We exchanged glances. Was The Queen in labor? Was she all right? Had she given birth?

Tackett bid us follow him to the giant parlor. "We'll wait here for news!"

The royal family, several dozen of them, had gathered together, waiting. They chatted nervously but happily with each other. Their attire was Sunday's best. We felt plainly dressed in our every-day play clothes. At least we had been sanitized.

More pigs continued to arrive. Each one beautifully dressed. An abundance of food and fruit drinks were being served on ornate golden trays by young, light blue male pigs like Handel. They too wore long black, split tail coats.

I stood near a large yellow pig who looked motherly. I waited until she looked at me and smiled before asking her a question.

"Is it The Queen? Does anyone know yet how she is?"

"Yes, it is The Queen. Her Highness is getting old, but she is in the best of health. I am Dot. Glory Rose is my sister. Our mother was Rose Queen, Sana Rose, who died when we were five years old. My sister is a good Queen. We all adore her."

"Will someone tell us when a baby is born?" Laura asked.

Good question. All of us were dying to know.

"See that little balcony at the top of the stairs? One of her attendants will stand there and give us word." Dot told us. "She always has eight pigs."

Every now and then I wanted to pinch myself, thinking I must surely wake up from this dream. It had to be a dream! I said it to myself over and over.

Tackett told us that the elves were in the auditorium, waiting for news. A messenger would rush them word as soon as a baby was born.

All eyes turned to the balcony where a pretty, young, lavender pig took center stage.

"Her Highness, Queen Glory Rose has given birth to a white male baby."

The family smiled and applauded, but kept on talking to each other. It was a festive occasion.

"What do you bet me, girls?" Billy grinned. "Will she, or will she not have a pink pig with a red rose painted on its butt?"

"If I had a daisy, I'd be plucking off the petals asking, will she or will she not," Laura declared.

"The answer never comes out right," her sister told her.

Not more than two minutes passed when another young aide stood on the balcony. This one was pale gold. She smiled happily, signifying all was well with The Queen.

"Her Highness, our beloved Queen Glory Rose has given birth to two babies, light green in color. One is male and one is female.

"That makes three," I counted. "Come on, little Rose Princess! Where are you? We are waiting for you."

A nurse came down the stairs and walked directly to us. We felt embarrassed. The pigs stared.

"Her Majesty asks that you remain today as long as you can. She hopes to see you in about an hour." The tall white nurse smiled down at us, waiting for an answer.

"Thank you," we all replied, telling her we had several hours yet before we had to leave.

The nurse had a golden ring in her nose and a pearl dangling from the ring. But, no matter how she decorated it, it was still the nose of a hog. I had to laugh. Don't start laughing now, I told myself. Doctors! White pigs in white coveralls! A nurse with a ring in her nose! All walking on their hind legs, talking, educated. Wow! I said to myself, "Self, behave!"

When the food tray came by again, the food looked familiar, small sandwiches and punch, just like it came from Missouri. So I helped myself. And, darned if it didn't taste like Missouri. Not meat sandwiches, but more like butter flavored with herbs. Delicious.

There was another announcement, about another pig. It was not pink.

The elves had arrived. They too were beautifully dressed in honor or the occasion. Whatever the next few minutes brought, good or bad, they wanted to be on hand.

Babies five and six were yellow and the seventh was another white male.

The grand parlor became deathly silent. Smiles vanished. One whisper from a young pig brought her stares of criticism.

The four of us stood close together, heads bowed, fingers crossed, promising God all kinds of things if he would use his influence to bring forth a miracle. After all of the things I had heard in Sunday School that God could do, a pink pig should be a snap.

After a long five minutes baby number eight was born, an auburn female. The Queen's sister had told us that Glory Rose always had eight. So, it was over!

What would we tell Ernie? Would he ever recover?

Chapter 21. A Small Miracle

After the eighth pig was born, tears flowed freely.

A few members of the royal family left the room, but only a few. The rest stood around in groups consoling each other. They were devastated, their future uncertain.

The elves' reaction was that of great reverence. Forming small circles, perhaps families, they held hands, bowed on one knee and lowered their heads as if in prayer. Not even the youngest of them uttered a sound out of respect for their beloved Queen.

An unexpected voice spoke from the balcony. "We bid you greetings." We were startled by a deep voice. There stood three men, ---humans! They wore long brown robes, and were old, but very handsome looking.

"Wait upon your Queen and pledge to her your loyalty. For on this day she has given birth to a ninth baby, a new heir. One who will hold the keys to all the powers bestowed upon this unending line of royalty since the very beginning. The babe will be known as Princess Rose Maria until the day The Queen Mother journeys back to us. And then Rose Maria will become your Queen. What say ye?"

A joyous shout rang forth from the waiting crowd. All the pigs and all the elves together recited, "Hail Great Queen, heir of magic. Good health. Long life. We pledge thee our honor. Hail to thee!"

We would have said it too, but we didn't know the words.

We joined hands and danced round and round. We laughed, cried and hugged each other.

The three men turned and vanished. The shouts and applause were deafening.

A band of musicians rushed in from an adjoining room. Had they waited there for this moment? Probably. There was about a dozen of them, ruddy, round faced little men and beautiful little women. All dressed in pink for the occasion. Red roses had been embroidered on the backs and fronts of their long satin coats for this special celebration.

The party was in full swing. More pigs, all ages and colors, continued to pour into the large hall.

From the parlor we could see the great dining room. The Primer Pots were getting a workout to feed the entire city.

The little people had their own style of merry making. They sang and shouted and hugged each other, as we had done. Some turned cartwheels. Some walked upside down on their hands. They weren't any taller upside down than they were right side up.

Another part of the ballroom was opened up to accommodate everyone. The elves paraded with their musicians and clowns. I wondered if we could expect the dweeds. They were no doubt laying in wait someplace, to surprise us.

A Queen's attendant came for us. We giggled all the way up those marbled stairsteps. We were the first to be invited up. And we felt special!

The medics had gone.

Her Highness was propped up on a white velvet chaise lounge. Beside her was a tiny pink wicker basket---Oh my gosh! It looked just like a miniature Transit Basket, except it did not have a door on the side. It was open from the top like a regular baby's bed.

The little pink Princess lay sleeping in the basket. Her little red rose was in plain view.

"Isn't she wonderful, children?" The Queen smiled.

We were in awe of the new heir. It was hard to believe how tiny she was when The Queen was so large, probably a good 400 pounds. The baby weighed, at the most, three pounds.

"Our magic will not be taken from us, children. Did you hear the Ancient Elders?" she asked.

Laura's eyes opened wide, "Is that who they were?" she exclaimed.

"They sure were old!" Billy added seriously.

"They are many hundreds of years old, Billy," The Queen said, proudly.

"We came back to give you a report about the gardens. Now, you have no use for them. It's better this way. This is your way and I'm sure it's the right way for your kingdom, but not for ours." I said to her.

"We were worried about the gardens. The soil is so poor the vegetables look terrible, but outside in the garbage containers, the worms have turned the soil into pure gold. The few seed we planted out there are growing great and healthy looking," Iva shared.

Billy had a favor to ask. "Your Highness, when those green beans we planted outside are ready to eat, would you please eat some of them? I know you'll like them. And when you eat them will you think of us? Those seeds were from Missouri."

"Of course, Billy. I promise I will. But I won't have to eat the beans to think of you children. I will never forget you, for coming to a strange land, trusting us, and yes, coming to our rescue." Glory Rose had a tear in her eye. "I did not bargain on caring so much for all of you."

Iva looked squarely at The Queen. "Now we can tell you about Ernie."

"I knew you were keeping something from me," she said. "How is the boy?"

"Ernie is very ill. He loves you and has worried himself sick about your problem. Now we can go back and tell him about Princess Rose Maria. He'll get better in no time!" Iva felt certain.

"I can do better than that!" she smiled a broad happy smile. "Let's take the Princess to Ernie!"

"What! Do you really mean it?" Billy cried.

We were a happy bunch of kids, even though we didn't know exactly what she meant. Where would she take the Princess?

"In the morning I will bring her. We shall meet you at the spot where you board the Transit Basket. Bring the boy and we will make him well again," The Queen predicted.

"We will be there with Ernie at ten o'clock." I promised.

Iva, Laura, Billy and I each got to hold the beautiful pink princess. We kissed her on the head and felt of the tiny red rose on her right hip. Then we bid The Queen good-bye until tomorrow and told her how happy we were that her problems were over.

The celebrating down stairs was loud and jolly. The royal family members and elves were lined up, all the way to the top of the stairs to see the baby.

We sensed we might never see them again. Saying our good-byes, we headed home. We always managed to get back in time, for fear of being found out. We stepped from one world into another.

For me it was time for chores and supper. My friends hurried home to share the good news with their brother.

Later that night, my dad and I went horse back riding around Watson. Ernie was in his yard playing with Billy and the Case kids. His big smile said it all. He had heard the news. I hollered at him to say hello.

"How ya doing, Ernie?" I shouted.

"I'm pretty good, thank you," he grinned.

Daddy and I both felt better about Ernie. We rode by our friends' houses and said "hello" to those who were either working or sitting in their yards. Evelyn Martin was visiting her sister, Alma Gaines.

So many people had helped out with Ernie: the Harmons, Garsts, Leismans, Jochims, a couple of Gaines families, Fredes, Sharps, Morgans, Maupins, Stantons and countless others. Yes, Watson was an o.k. place to live. We made our own special magic.

Iva managed to get Ernie away from her mother the next morning in time to keep our special appointment. Elsie noticed Ernie was much better, so she was willing to let him go.

I didn't want to give my mother an opportunity to say we should not play in the cellar that morning, so I thought long and hard about how I would talk to her.

"We'll only play in the cellar for a little while this morning," I said. "Ernie wants to. He's better and he hasn't played down there for a couple of weeks!"

"Anything that makes that little fellow happy is fine with me," Mama said, just as I hoped she would.

Finally, ten o'clock arrived I gathered up a few pictures to show The Queen. Ernie began to grin. He walked down the cellar steps and stared at the door.

Tackett was on time. Tackett had always been on time. He greeted Ernie and began to laugh.

"Guess what The Queen's first order of business was this morning?"

"What? what?" we asked.

"The first order of business was to recarpet those garden spots." He held his belly and laughed some more, and we laughed with him.

"We knew that would happen, didn't we?" he said to us. We surely did. That was exactly what our squeaky clean Queen would do.

We hurried down the hallway to the Transit Basket.

The little Princess stood on the soft seat next to her mother. She stepped closer to her mother when we approached them.

"Don't be shy, Rose Marie," The Queen smiled proudly at all of us. "There is someone very special who has been ill. He wants to meet you."

Iva pushed Ernie closer. The Queen picked up the little Rose Princess and placed her in Ernie's outstretched arms.

Ernie took a deep breath. Tears trailed down his cheeks. "She is so-o beautiful, Your Hineyness," he blubbered through his tears of joy. "I have never seen anything so pretty. And she's magic! I sure wish I was magic!"

We had to laugh at Ernie when he called The Queen Your Hineyness. Her Highness laughed too.

While Ernie held the baby, I showed The Queen a picture of our hogs. She chuckled.

"They look just like my ancestors," she said, "without tusks!"

I showed her a picture of my Dad and Mother. She studied the pictures for several minutes.

"How different we are," she said. "But even though we are different, difference does not matter. We can still love each other."

Billy asked the question we all had on our minds. "Where is your kingdom, anyway? Where were we?"

The Queen answered with a tear in her eye. "Well, my friends, it's a place you have to be very young to find."

"I love you guys," Ernie told The Queen as he handed the baby back to her mother.

"And I love you, Ernie, and you, Billy, and you, Laura, and you, Iva, and you, Colene." We all cried. She was leaving and we would never see her again. We had come to the end of something very wonderful.

Tackett wiped his eyes and touched the little Orb on his hat. At that moment we found ourselves sitting in the cellar on fruit boxes. The door was gone.

The Ellison kids and I were content. The Queen's kingdom would live on in a manner to which they had become accustomed. And Ernie, well, Ernie grew up to be a very healthy, handsome man.

And we all lived happily, ever after.

The End

Epilogue

Many years later, I sat with my father as he lay dying. He reached for my hand.

"Colene," he said weakly. "There is something I want to tell you, something I have never told anyone, not even your mother."

Daddy grew up on our farm with his parents. He too played in the cellar when he was a small child.

"When I was ten years old," he continued, "I had the strangest dreams! At least I think they were dreams. I dreamed I walked right through our cellar wall to a place where a pig Queen reigned over elves. Her name was Rose Anne. She became very ill and I was sent for. One of them had learned that by vaccinating our hogs we made them well. I took vaccine from our vet to the palace to make The Queen well. They had no doctors or hospitals."

"They do now, Dad," I told him, "they do now!"

He smiled at me and squeezed my hand, satisfied in knowing that I too had been there. To a place where only children go.

Queen Glory Rose was right. She was a very intelligent lady. It was she who said, "To find a magic place, you have to be very young!"